"Miss, I'm sorry. I know you aren't from around here. I didn't recognize the boy, and I just jumped to conclusions."

She stared him down, her hair a butterscotch waterfall draped down her back. Then, like a passing storm, she smiled at him, and he was hooked like a brook trout. Every curve of her long body showed their finest angles as dripping clothes melded to tanned skin.

Tad felt a forgotten longing stir that resulted in a tightening of his wet jeans. She noticed as a naughty grin replaced her warm smile. Her good-natured laughter filled the air, as rich as the river's rush.

"You definitely jumped, anyway. Here." She handed him the towel and rousted her hair with both hands. "It was a tense, hot minute, that's for sure. I knew I wouldn't reach him in time, but I had to try. I didn't know there were rude superheroes lurking and jumping."

She reached out to take her towel back and held out her manicured hand for him to shake, a few water droplets shimmering on white-tipped fingernails.

"Look, it was a misunderstanding, already forgiven. I'm Jaime Summers. My friend Lana owns this resort, and she hired me for the summer to…" she trailed off. "What?"

He didn't shake her hand, resentment kindling. Jaime Summers was trouble. Lug's disappearing daughter, she had moved to Riverbend Falls as a kid after he left for college and from what he could gather, she'd brought trouble with her. Now Trouble was back and hot as an August afternoon.

He sent up a silent prayer, hoping she was not *that* Jaime Summers.

Dear Reader,

Summer holidays are the best! I'm so pleased the majestic views of Riverbend Falls will grace your summer days. The night sky will light up with a dazzling display of fireworks, the smell of bar-b-ques will fill the air, and the sound of splashing will be everywhere! I hope you relish the chance to read about Jaime and Tad's slice of life and find it as amusing and entertaining as I do. Jaime brings the party when she's back in town.

Jaime is feisty and unapologetic, but when she jumps into a family setting with both feet, she considers impressionable young minds, and it changes her outlook on life—though not necessarily her personality.

Tad is charming and stubborn. I like a man who knows what he wants and is up front about it. I respect what it takes to be a single parent, and his determination humbles me.

Jaime and Tad are struggling to find solutions to the problems they face. I love the way they team up, working their way through the idea of being friends. Or more…

I'd love to hear from you! Check-in at delilahsdiction.com and sign up for my newsletter! While you're there, follow me on Pinterest to see the photos I use to inspire me, or at my Facebook page, where I enjoy "Sharing My Journey" with each of you!

Delilah

Planting Jasmine

Riverbend Falls ~ Book 2

Delilah Dewey

ISBN: 979-8-9873319-2-7 (Paperback)
Library of Congress Control Number: 2023908011

PLANTING JASMINE

Printed on Demand in the United States of America.

First printing, 2023.

Delilah's Diction
delilahsdiction@gmail.com

www.delilahsdiction.com

Dedication

To those of You who believed in me all along,
I know You. I love You.
Thank You!

This has been a wild journey, and many of you have had positive influences on my writing. I'm so thankful for the friends I've made during my life who gave me a boost or sent 'you can do it!' vibes. Thanks for being you!

To writers and readers who've shared their writing and life experiences with me, thank you for being an inspiration.

To my street team, you rock! Thank you for all you do.

ProWritingAid and Canva, thank you for creating software and sharing it so freely, making it possible to do what I do!

I especially want to thank my family for dealing with my wild ideas, thought-filled silences, and my plethora of scattered notes. Thanks for listening endlessly about my characters, and offering unwavering support and understanding of my eccentric behavior, which I'm claiming is a side effect of being a writer. I love every one of you. Thanks for accepting me just the way I am!

Chapter 1

"My niece would be a perfect match for you, Tad. She got rid of her no-good husband a few years ago. She'd help you raise those boys of yours. I told her what a hero you were this past winter when our apartments caught fire and you saved my cats." The widow Goodwin's dentures made a clink as her face lit up with a smile. Then she looked him over like he was for sale, and her nose scrunched in disapproval at his clothes.

Tad wanted to roll his eyes, but didn't. He appreciated the wisdom of his elders and had kindly listened to the same story five times in the last hour. Tad was over it, but he was partial to this tough old gal. He had helped her and her cats out of a burning building, but it was lucky timing, that was all.

Women weren't a priority for him, even if he had a free moment. The disaster that was his marriage still stung. He'd gone the full distance, but… no thank you. Problem was, plenty of folks had someone he should marry, but no one who was available to work. If he was going to float a fishing business on the side, he'd need help at the ranch.

"Calvin, Ryan, and I get along fine, Miz Goodwin. I could use a ranch hand, though, if you know of anyone looking for a job?"

He glanced down past his holey T-shirt and faded jeans. No dung on his boots, that was good. Despite most of the community showing up dressed out, he'd seen no reason to change. This was a workday with a break in it for him.

"I don't suppose I do." She eyeballed the shelves of canned jellies and jams before her and eventually chose a jar, lifting it up to the light to inspect it. "You know the youngsters, always in a hurry to move off and make it big."

She shot him a look, clearly assigning him some of that blame. She cast her gaze over the dwindling groups of people wandering around the renovated grain mill.

The smell of fresh-baked cookies and a whiff of sawdust wafted in the air as she said, "Maybe this place will encourage more of y'all to stay in the area. Tad, now you let me know if you want to meet my little Denise." She patted his cheek with a frail but firm hand and ambled off with her jar of jelly, muttering, "I don't reckon she's exactly little anymore…"

Excellent time to escape.

With a sigh of nostalgia, he left the old building where he had grown up playing secret agent. His boys had both disappeared about five minutes ago and Tad hoped they hadn't gone rogue. He saw his two minis kneeling beside the bench out front, soaking up stories and watching the old timers whittle on sticks.

Couple of good guys. Ed Rosati owned of one of the two restaurants in town, or had, until the Falls Mill empire descended on the old mill. Garrett and Lana, his sister and her new man, put in a restaurant upstairs, built a tavern downstairs, and planned some kind of breakfast bar, if they could figure out logistics. There was no telling where the madness would stop.

The other fella on the bench was a grizzled army vet, Lug Summers. He'd settled in at the edge of town after Tad left for college and beyond, so Tad didn't know him well.

Story was his family all cut out on him several years back. The fella might get a little deep into his cups now and then, but the stories he told fascinated Calvin. Kid would probably go military.

Tad wasn't sure the stories were PG enough for kids, but so far, he hadn't heard swearing in the retellings. He knew it was coming, though. The things Dads had to worry about.

He'd tasted soap plenty in his day. Not that it helped, but it made an impression.

His boys wouldn't miss him for at least twenty minutes. He'd parked his ancient Ford pickup—Ry had dubbed it the Green Beast—near the boat landing above the dam. It would be a perfect quiet spot for just a few minutes. Just to collect himself. Life hadn't slowed in six months, and he saw no end in sight. A second of peace would be just the thing. Almost at his sanctuary, he stopped, staring.

Down at the boat landing, an exotic creature stood in the sun about calf deep in the river's current, looking like she was alone in the world, despite the small child playing just upriver from her a bit. She sure wasn't a local.

Her sheer baby blue tee did little to hide a perky figure and a barely there skirt wrapped around a cute bottom, offering a study on long legs. Cables of hair, a riot of honeyed hues, shimmered in the sunlight. Long lashes hid her eyes, and with her face lifted to the sun, sultry lips open slightly, it seemed she was waiting for a kiss.

He turned away from the mother and her son. He had enough going on at the moment, as he'd spent the last hour making clear. Despite the odd thrill he felt when he saw her, he considered the bullet dodged.

A sudden panicked scream filled the air, and Tad swung back toward the water. The little boy was bobbing toward the millrace! He was keeping his head above water for now, but in about a minute, the commanding pull of water that powered the old mill's waterwheel would suck him in like a leaf.

A girl emerged from the trees along the bank and was screaming at the boy. His mom was struggling to walk toward him through the deepening water, but her progress was slow. She might reach him.

Then she lost her balance and fell in the water, dunking under, swimming for the boy as soon as she surfaced. He had too much of a lead. She wouldn't make it.

He snatched his hat off his head and threw it. In record time, he kicked his boots off and was running sock footed toward the millrace. He knew every inch of this section of the river and knew where the current was pushing the hardest.

Tad dove over the rushing water into the back eddy on the other side. Both of his knees hit bottom where it was too shallow, but he reached out in time to pluck the small boy back into the safety of the slower moving water.

Trying to catch his breath, he lifted the boy of about three into his arms and began the upstream trek around the current, getting more ticked off by the minute. This could have been his son. He didn't even have a life jacket on.

The two women were crossing to meet him, the younger one hysterical. The boy's sister, perhaps. When they met out in the water, the rush from the race was still pretty loud, but he let the mother have it.

"You weren't even watching your kid. That was totally irresponsible. Standing there, soaking in the sun like you didn't have a care in the world. It's not my business, lady, but you might try being a little less self-centered when someone this young and innocent depends on you." Mad is what he was. "Next time, put a life jacket on him before indulging yourself."

The hottie just stared at him, a wounded look in her aquamarine eyes.

He put the boy down, who splashed over to his sister. More to comfort her, Tad thought, as she was still half hysterical. The tyke seemed unfazed by his brush with death.

The sister stood up, wiping shame filled eyes and said, "I will. He was right in front of me and I only closed my eyes for a minute." She reached down and took the little boy's hand. "Thank you so much! You saved my little man. Can we repay you with a home cooked meal?"

Tad looked at the woman he'd been yelling at, confused. She shrugged, and her wet clothes did interesting things to her frame.

"Sorry, handsome, guessed wrong. I don't know these people."

She turned and walked out of the water toward the landing and stopped at the river's edge, grabbing a small towel from a pile of stuff on the bank. He looked down at the boy's real mom, young and wearing a bright pink tell-all bikini.

"No, thanks." Man, that was embarrassing. "Just get a life jacket on the kid, all right?"

Tad felt like he'd run a marathon as he stepped out on the boat landing, being careful not to bust his butt on the slick, mossy bottom. He considered the dive he'd made. Thankfully, his boys hadn't seen the reckless stunt.

He stepped lightly over to where his boots lay. Skinned knees were his prize, and without shoes, he'd bruised more than his ego walking across the riverbed. But these were his favorite boots. If he had jumped in with them, he probably would have drowned.

Content that he saved the boy and his boots, he snagged his lucky ball cap and snugged it onto his wet head, glancing over at the ticked off siren toweling off. He owed her an apology, at least. Carrying his boots, he stepped toward her despite the wicked glare she aimed at him.

"Miss, I'm sorry. I know you aren't from around here. I didn't recognize the boy, and I just jumped to conclusions."

She stared him down, her hair a butterscotch waterfall draped down her back. Then, like a passing storm, she smiled at him, and he was hooked like a brook trout.

Every curve of her long body showed their finest angles as dripping clothes melded to tanned skin. Tad felt a forgotten longing stir that resulted in a tightening of his wet jeans. She noticed as a naughty grin replaced her warm smile. Her good-natured laughter filled the air, as rich as the river's rush.

"You definitely jumped, anyway. Here." She handed him the towel and rousted her hair with both hands. "It was a tense, hot minute, that's for sure. I knew I wouldn't reach him in time, but I had to try. I didn't know there were rude superheroes lurking and jumping."

She reached out to take her towel back and held out her manicured hand for him to shake, a few water droplets shimmering on white-tipped fingernails. "Look, it was a misunderstanding, already forgiven. I'm Jaime Summers. My friend Lana owns this resort, and she hired me for the summer to…" she trailed off. "What?"

He didn't shake her hand, resentment kindling. Jaime Summers was bad news. Lug's disappearing daughter, she had moved to Riverbend Falls as a kid after he left for college and from what he could gather, she'd brought trouble with her. His sister was getting arrested with Jaime the night his parents died. Kat had been there, too, but he'd known her all his life. She was pretty level-headed.

Tad had a disturbing thought as he remembered agreeing to let Lana use his cottage for her summer contractor. She'd claimed her cabins were all booked to capacity for most of the season. Now Trouble was back and hot as an August afternoon.

He sent up a silent prayer, hoping she was not *that* Jaime Summers.

This smile was slow and sassy, correctly interpreting his silence. He briefly wondered how many smiles she had. Oh, man.

"My reputation precedes me then… no worries, I'll not lead away the children of the town with my pied piper whistle."

She gathered her shirt away from her skin to wring the water from it, giving him a perfect view of her exquisite breasts wrapped in a low-cut bra. Also tan. Well.

"Oh, for heaven's sake, stop looking at me like that. I don't know you, mister, and you sure don't know me. Obviously." Her tirade cut short when she glanced over his shoulder up the landing. "Just great. It figures." She gave Tad a glare that held more fury than he warranted, since he hadn't said anything yet.

Tad turned to find his sons standing at the top of the landing, getting an eyeful of a tall, nearly naked wet woman and their dad ogling her. Naturally, standing between his boys with an intimidating scowl directed at them both, was Lug Summers, Jaime's dad.

Jaime glanced over Tad's shoulder at the remodeled historic mill and debated her choices. Her best friend needed her help, but this was not a promising beginning. She was here to do a job, and she could do that. She would not climb back in to her sunny yellow Volkswagen and drive away from this backwater sluice of memories.

Did it have to be in Riverbend Falls? She'd sworn she'd never come back. There would be endless torments during the muggy, miserable summer. And bugs. Yuck. Lana had saved her bum dozens of times, though. Lana needed her particular skill set and moral support, unless she misjudged the last conversation.

She had hoped to avoid her dad until she was ready to deal with him. As if there would ever be time for that. Stubborn old…

Jaime daydreamed about mending fences with her dad too often to dwell on. Now the scenarios were blown out of the water, literally. Jaime was wet, barefoot—and embarrassed. With a quick glance at the extremely sexy, very rude dude who must know she single-handedly destroyed this small town's innocence, she focused on the scowling figure and the two small boys. She didn't know who they were, or why her dad would hold their hands. Her VW was just about 30 paces away…

"Dad?!" Both Jaime and the older boy said the word, and she realized this broody, sexy cowpoke must be their father. Great. She would get wet over a stud with kids.

Her dad's expression was stern and uninviting. His steely eyes assessed her half-dressed soaked state, and he spoke instead to the boy's father.

"Tad, Cal & Ry here are on a mission for ice cream. Lana is ready to spoil 'em, but I told them they'd have to ask you. I'm headed out." Then he left without another word.

Her dad had just ignored her, and that hurt more than the fight she'd expected. Now he had the upper hand. It still wasn't too late to make a break for it. The two boys came down the hill with their eyes glued to her and she felt unusually conscious of her wet t-shirt contest winning figure.

No matter what she did, the reunion with Lug after ten years was a bust, as she'd embarrassed him again. He didn't have to be proud of her, just acknowledge she'd made it on her own.

Now he wouldn't be thinking it looked like she had a plan at all. Hmph.

She watched him drive away and glanced at Tad, feigning boredom. "Tad, huh? Being a small town, and what I know about Lana's family, it's my luck that you're my landlord for the summer. Is that right, handsome?"

Camouflage eyes considered her, and she felt like a fish on a line. Eat it or throw it back.

"If you're Lana's summer contractor, I guess I'm that landlord."

He said the words so reluctantly, Jaime's embarrassment heightened. Men did not treat her like the plague. Ever. But she supposed he had every reason to hate her.

"Lana said it'd be no problem… I know you don't rent out your cabin, so thanks. I won't be a bother, and it's only for the summer. I was a girl scout…" Jaime realized she was babbling and the two youngsters were peering up at her with big eyes. "I'll just hit the grocery for some grub and I'll be set. So, I better get going."

"Girl Scout, huh?" He gave her rhinestone shoes a snarky glance. "The grocery store is closed. The town turned out for Community Day."

She snagged the silly slippers—she knew she needed water shoes; they were just packed—and slipped her wet tender feet in, eager to be on her way. Anywhere.

"I didn't think of that." She swore, then looked down at the boys holding their dad's hands, and their eyes widened again. She covered her mouth. "I mean, darn."

Then she felt herself turning red. That was worse. Man. Tad was staring at her, completely amused despite his earlier antagonism. Well… she'd felt his disapproval, even if he hadn't said so.

"I've got snacks. I'll make it just fine." She was a chef. She could figure out what to do with a half bag of peanuts and a chocolate bar, surely. "You guys will barely know I'm there." The room and board was on somebody else's dime, and she'd have precious privacy for gaming nights. "It was nice meeting you all. I'll just pop in and let Lana know I made it."

Before she chickened out and left.

Lana had asked her brother to let her use the cabin, but she must not have given him all the details. She hadn't told Jaime he had his kids with him, or that he was holding a grudge. Tad knew *of* her. She had seen name recognition flare in his eyes when she introduced herself.

Good thing she loved her best friend unconditionally.

Jaime started away from the little family. Tad could be as unfriendly as he wanted. She rarely made friends, so he didn't matter. He was just a landlord. If the summer went the way she thought it would, she'd be at the restaurant all the time, so his lack of manners wouldn't even affect her.

"So, you were an actual Girl Scout?"

She glanced over her shoulder and saw they were following her, an interested expression on Tad's handsome face. Jaime's lust meter trembled a bit. Fool.

"Yeah, well…" She paused with a half turn, lifting her damp hair off her neck. "I haven't thought of that in years. I guess I'll be glad I earned my hospitality badges, staying around here."

Her trunk with her stuff wasn't due to be delivered until tomorrow. It shouldn't have been a problem. She'd just cruised on into the campground turned resort, knowing they'd had a huge opening Memorial weekend and had dedicated this last day for the community to come down and check out the progress.

"All the stores are closed, like, everywhere?" Panic must have shown on her face, because his smile seemed genuine. Maybe he was on medications or something making him irrational.

"Look, Miss Summers, we got off on the wrong foot." He waved his boots at her with a grin, but he seemed to be arguing with himself. The war of it spread across his dark, woodsy features. His dark mustache worked up and down as he obviously tried to plan something less rude to say.

"I reckon the boys and I are planning to hunt down Lana and finagle some ice cream. After that, we're heading to the house. If you want to tag along, we can show ya around, get ya settled in, and make sure you don't starve before the grocery store opens. We'll be throwing some burgers on the grill about suppertime."

His voice reminded Jaime of her favorite vodka, a creamy warmth with a citrus bite, and she was tempted… mostly tempted to tell him to kiss off just to spite him, but she'd love a quick visit with Lana and a chance to settle in, and there was a raid tonight. A nap before she joined sounded like heaven. The trip wore her nerves to a frazzle, and seeing her dad before she was ready had fried what little patience she had left.

"Fine, thanks," she said, not sure about any of this.

"Boys, this girl scout is Miss Jaime Summers, Aunt Lana's friend. Miss Jaime is the lady who's going to be staying in your clubhouse for the next few months. Do you boys mind if we invite her to have ice cream with us?"

"Okay with us." The older boy said.

"Will you boys introduce yourselves?" Tad asked.

"Uhm, okay." Solemn eyes a shade grayer than his dad's peered at her as the older boy stuck out a small hand. "Pleased to meet you, Miss Jaime. My name's Cal, and this is Ry. It's not our entire names, but Dad let us pick what we like and we like to say it like the ballplayers. Ma'am." He gave an extra good pump with the last word, and Jaime's heart went a little soft.

"Well, boys, I like your names very much. I dig baseball."

"You know about baseball?" Cal looked at her doubtfully and she tweaked his frayed cap.

"Sure do, sport. My dad taught me everything there is to know." The thought had her hesitating, missing the simple ease she'd had with her dad when they'd talked sports. It had been just their thing, since her twin wasn't into it, but that was a long time ago.

"So, I'm invited to come have some ice cream with you, huh?" She shot a quick glance at Tad, but there was no trace of his earlier hostility, or his attraction, for that matter. "You say you know where I can find your cool Aunt Lana?"

"Yep, yep!" The boys bounced and squealed, leading the way up the boat ramp, back toward the newly christened Falls Mill

Bar and Grill. Tad cast her damp miniskirt and shirt a dubious look.

"Luckily for me, this heat is outrageous, and I'm nearly dry." She gave her tee another airy shake, willing it to dry faster. She had one duffel, and it had in it a swimsuit—which she could have used a minute ago—an oversized tee to sleep in, and a change of clothes to start work in tomorrow.

With two children hanging around, Jaime felt seriously self-conscious, and there was nothing to be done for it. She looped her meager wet towel over her shoulders and wondered what was next.

Chapter 2

"Jasmine Summers, as I live and breathe!" Lana's cheeks were glowing. She was into the dude next to her, clearly the new hubby. And was that a baby bump? Her Lana, man-hater Lana?

Judging by the love-struck man at her side, they had come to terms with their original doubts about compatibility. She grinned. Lana spent half the girls' lives trying to convince everyone she'd no plans for love, and now? Fabulously in love.

"Lana, my dear, you look amazing." Jaime studied her best friend before hugging her tight. She leaned back and laughed, and rubbed Lana's nose for luck, a silly thing they had done as girls. "I can't believe the changes. This place is impressive."

"Garrett, honey, this is the infamous Jasmine Summers. She's going to help us wrestle down the crazy that is ramping up here at Fall's Mill. The new name sounds so relaxing, but Jaime, honestly I'm hoping you can work some magic when it comes to staffing, because after the weekend we had, I don't know how long until I remember what the word relax feels like."

"We'll see what we can do." Jaime laughed and stuck her hand out to shake Garrett's. "Well, it's nice to meet you, man. I thought you might resemble Shrek the way Lana fussed about you when you first met."

"She treated me like an ogre, there's no doubt, but I won over my sweet Fiona." He draped his arms around Lana with a grin, hugging her from behind as she rolled her eyes. "Glad to have you on board. I've heard a lot about you."

"All good, I hope." Jaime offered casually, trying not to care. No way it was all good. Lana didn't fault her for injecting some fun into this boring town, but the other locals had heard stories and rightly blamed her for that night. Obviously including Tad. Too bad.

"Garrett, honey, would you get Ry and Cal some ice cream?" Lana gave Tad a considering grin. "I'm scared to ask why you are sopping wet and carrying your boots, so like a dutiful sister, I'm going to ignore it." She turned to Jaime and motioned her to a side door. "I'm taking Jaime out to show off the new deck."

The open house had apparently been a success. Mostly eaten appetizer trays lay discarded on the bar. The few folks still dwindling were talking about hay fields and crop ratios.

Then Ryan spoke up, a little loud. "Miss Jaime wants mint chocolate chip, right?" The kid looked at her expectantly with eyes the same bright blue as his grandpa had had.

Jaime's legendary hard heart melted. "I definitely do." Kid beamed at her, and she smiled back, feeling humbled. On the short walk over to the mill, the boys had talked over each other, telling her about the little league team they were playing on this summer and pumped her for her favorite flavors of ice cream while they shared all of theirs.

Tad barely spoke during the short walk, picking his footing carefully, letting the children carry the conversation. He probably busted the fool out of his shins with that heroic leap from nowhere. He was a pretty good sport, though, not whining about it. Her feet hurt from the short stroll she'd taken across the river's bottom. She'd never say a word.

She hadn't wanted to come back, but the boredom she feared didn't seem like it was going to be a problem. She'd been in town less than an hour and intense was a better description.

"You got it, kiddo. You guys want triple dips? We'll go up to the Clubhouse and make the cones, on our way back down, you can deliver to the ladies, then we'll look for fish in the millrace."

Garrett herded the boys toward the resort office where the hand dipped ice cream kiosk was and Jaime overheard him say, "Get to do any fishing this week, Tad? And I totally want to hear why you and the new girl are both wet."

Jaime didn't think anyone noticed when she and Lana pushed out the lounge door onto the lofty deck overlooking the man-made waterfall. She grinned at Lana. "I bet you want to know, too, but you're too nice to ask."

Lana slapped her arm. "I'm not too nice. What is going on with you two?"

"Nothing. He's got kids, sheesh. You know I have standards." Jaime leaned over the porch railing. The river was breathtaking from this vantage point. "Lucy, you got some 'splaining to do… so yeah, we've met. He's heard enough to not want me around, no doubt."

Lana shrugged, looking sheepish.

"I can't believe I let you talk me into this." Jaime was sulking. She wanted sympathy. Except for getting to see Lana, there were no perks to this gig, and she had no idea how she was going to survive the summer in this town. "Remind me why I'm doing this. It sounded reasonable a few weeks ago."

Lana laughed heartily, throwing her arm around Jaime's neck. "Because you love me. I'm guessing by your indignant tone you and my brother didn't exactly hit it off? I'd hoped to introduce you, figures he found you first. He's had a lot on his mind with the boys moving in with him this summer. He remembered you were staying up at his place?"

Jaime pushed at her damp curls and leaned over the top rail with a huff. Without her blow dryer to straighten them, her curls would coil like medusa's snakes.

"Oh, he remembered, and he's not too happy about it. You didn't tell him it was me? He's a jerk, ya know? He insulted me, refused to shake my hand, then invited me to ice cream. You two have real issues, ya know that?"

"Buck up, chickadee. You're here to save my bacon, possibly literally." Lana looked out over the water, a somber mode catching her.

"All right. So… mind blown. I can't believe what you've done here. It does not look like the same old drafty building we snuck around in as kids." It was so alive. Not how she remembered it.

"Man, it has been nuts. I won't lie. I really got going on Garrett's ideas—and he just kept funding me." Lana bumped her hip against Jaime's. "I think I upsold us a little more than I should of because we created a monster. I don't know if we can get a handle on this."

"Don't worry so much." Lana had anxiety shimmering in her emerald eyes, and Jaime knew she would do whatever Lana needed.

"I'll spare you the details until I get you on the clock, but the skeleton crew we've been working with through the winter is falling apart already, and, well… let's say, we're overwhelmed. I'm glad you came. I'll ask Tad to get you settled before I…"

"Are you positive there is nowhere else to stay?"

With a shrug, Lana said, "I booked our cabins solid most of the year, which I'm regretting, and definitely through the next three months. You could stay with us, but I know you said you needed your own space, and with the puppy and… are you sure you can only stay the summer?"

Jaime gave Lana her most confident smile. "I've got a line on a fabulous cruise ship for the winter months this year, and they need me as bad as you do. Don't worry, little sister, I'll have your people running themselves in three months. I don't think I'll be in danger of needing to stay on."

"If I had people," Lana muttered, then nodded. "Well, Tad's place is just up the hill, so it'll be convenient." Then that gleam lit behind her eyes again. "I just found out from Doc Robbins that I need to remodel the guest room I was working on at our place into a nursery."

"Oh! I thought maybe so! Well, no way I would intrude on a remodeling project, but let me know if I can lend a hand."

She laughed and clapped her hands a few times in jest. Jaime never had an itch for a kid, but watching Lana grow and thrive filled her with pride. She felt a warmth in her chest as joy filled her heart.

There was still Tad to deal with, though. "If I'm stuck with the renegade cowboy's cabin, I just need you to know, even for you, I won't take his sass. There's barely a manner in the boy. I guess everyone here hates me, but I don't plan to prove myself to anyone."

Lana sighed. "Everyone will love you, doll, because everybody does. They'll see you for the goodness that is you. Now you don't worry. I have a good feeling about this. You just do you, and it will magically convince people to do what you want them to. That just works for you. Now tell me you haven't already jumped in the river. You're a natural, Jaime. You've just got to give this town another chance. Did you jump in with my brother?"

"That's why I love you, babe. You always balance boring things like reason and rhyme and then… sneak attack." Jaime stared, fascinated, as a beautiful gray bird landed in the water. It was a long-legged fisher working just a few feet from where she'd slipped and fallen in the water. It caught a fish in its beak and lifted into the air. Like a nature show.

"Really, you should have seen him. He just jumped over the millrace like a superhero and saved some ladies' kid. It was, uhm… spectacular. But he is rude, and I don't truck with anyone ruder than me. That's my schtick."

She grinned at Lana and slapped her on her rump.

"But… since you love me just the way I am, I'll start tomorrow, and you can bring me up to speed. I'm going to have to drive to Branson and shop one day this week. My trunk is going to come tomorrow filled with my camping gear, but you have a much cooler thing going on here than the campground I remember. This is plush!" She giggled. She was going to be a part of this crazy new thing. At least for a minute.

Laughing, Lana patted her back. "I wish I could go, but I am not kidding. We are packed out for the rest of the summer, so I'll have to hang around. Look, Tad doesn't mean to be a jerk. He's just been under a lot of pressure lately, and all three of them are adjusting. I suspect you won't be up there except to sleep mostly, anyway. All the action is going to be here."

Lana leaned into Jaime and gave her arm a little squeeze. "Just try not to leave a trail of broken hearts around town, because you look plum delicious. You have been basking in the sun!"

"I have, and it was glorious." Jaime mimed chewing on hayseed, but she watched the waterfall spill over the dam, thinking. "I honestly doubt I'll find time to tumble into anyone's hay barn, darlin', but I promise if I do, I won't kiss and tell."

She might break a few hearts, but it wouldn't be her fault. She just always did.

Her pretty face was a commodity she traded in, but she liked to use her mind and her heart to figure out what made people tic. She took risks and then used all her assets.

Now she made good money working wherever she wanted. She'd just finished catering a two-week wedding on a cruise ship and walked away with a solid offer from the cruise line for a job to manage this winter's 25th anniversary celebration for its patrons. Big budget, three months tops, just the way she liked it.

She got itchy if she stayed in one place too long, and she'd discovered if she came into a business, took charge, and let everyone know she was teaching and leaving, she exacted much better results.

She got most of her business by word of mouth, and she was pleased with the reputation she'd built herself. It was lonely, though. Her Dad wouldn't speak to her until she conformed to his expectations, which was unlikely, and who knew what her free-spirited mother was doing. She knew her twin was unreachable. That hurt most, but he was soul searching or something.

Men… well, if she felt a connection, she offered a brief dalliance. When she moved on, she left her relationships behind, and she liked to be up front about it. She didn't always get what she wanted, but it was enough for her to maintain a respectable sex life. She'd learned the hard way, and it wasn't always simple, but it was by far the most efficient.

Pop! Tad caught the baseball in his glove as both his boys turned their attention to the door of his guest cabin. He waited for Cal to look back at him and returned the ball with an easy overhead arc. "Low and outside. But close. Just target the glove, and follow up with instinct."

"Dad, I'm tired of practicing pitching. Miss Jaime's coming out. Can I show her how I bat? I'm good at batting, Dad."

"I know ya are, sport. We can have Hydro shag balls. Grab the bat, then."

Cal laughed, his own hazel eyes shining from under his grubby White Sox cap. "Looks like Hydro likes her. She's super pretty, Dad. C'mon Ry, let's go save her."

Tad glanced at where his overgrown lab pup had lain intently, watching for a missed ball to slobber on. The only sign he'd been there was the wallow of earth where the dog had scratched out to stay cool. The hotter it got, the more holes he was getting in his yard.

Cal and Ry took off after Hydro, and he watched with a wince as his furball launched himself at his unsuspecting guest. Two front paws on her stomach, Hydro knocked Jaime flat on her butt, an expanse of tan legs stretching out in front of her. From the frightened screams she was emitting, she thought the dog was going to eat her.

It would take a while to convince her Hydro was harmless.

"Shoot, I'm the one who needs rescued." Tad followed his unruly mob across the yard, lifting his ball cap to push his hand through a mass of hair that still needed trimmed, and tucked his fidget tool firmly back on his head. Yep, this sassy woman was going to be a handful.

He would need to set ground rules for the kids, asap. She had joked about being the pied piper, but Tad had a real awareness of how impressionable and sensitive his children were, and they were already setting their hearts on this taboo chickee. Heck, she'd have every male from 6 to 60 crushing on her by the end of the week if she planned to work dressed like that.

If his sister and her man thought bringing Jaime on board was going to calm down the firestorm they'd started, they were dead wrong. Tad bet she had dedicated groupies by season's end wherever she worked on the place. The woman had some legs, and his thinking about them was going to mess up the stable routines he'd planned for this summer.

She was one of his sister's best friends, but her arrival was stirring up the rumor mill. Even just having Jaime out on his land this summer was going to have the busybodies hopping. Gossip that could get back to the boys, and he didn't want them getting the wrong idea.

His sis asking "can my summer contractor bunk in your cabin" and the real deal—can a smoking hot bad girl spend the summer—blew his mind. His sister was such an idealist. He studied Jaime watching his family's antics and wondered if it was possible to become an idealist.

He couldn't help but appreciate her long, toned legs, visible underneath her peculiar outfit. She'd put on a huge t-shirt with Garfield on it and knotted it at the waist, and still had on the short skirt. He guessed from the size of her duffel bag she hadn't brought a lot. He'd heard she spent time in rehab, and was glad not to see any evidence of substance abuse in her glowing skin and mischievous bright eyes.

Hydro approved of her, though she was giving him plenty of room as the boys showed off his obedience training. Obviously not muscle memory for the pup.

He shouldn't have invited Jaime to dinner, he still had to water the garden, and he'd meant to have tomorrow's hay already stacked on the truck for feeding in the morning, but the boys had talked him into practicing out back where they could watch the cabin.

His own curiosity would have him up a half hour earlier in the morning. But he was gracious. She'd be hungry. Even with the weird vibes between them, she'd show up, because she would like to be where the action was.

He was an avoid the action kind of guy, so hopefully he'd be able to keep his boys from falling in love. Just let her do her thing and move on. Or he might end up searching for answers to more of the torture questions.

"Dad, why can't we stay together? Dad, does Mommy love us? Daddy, can't you stay?"

That was behind him now. There were qualifications, there always were with his ex, but Tad wasn't worried. He proved he could handle anything for his boys.

He'd need to keep tabs on everything, though. Judith's skeptical nature was likely to spark over this, and it wouldn't help for Cal and Ry to get much more excited about the "super pretty" hot topic contractor.

"Your blonde cannonball just knocked me over and licked my face!" She wiped her gorgeous high cheekbones dramatically.

"Which one?" Tad asked, comically grinning suspiciously at the boys.

The boys giggled, and Jaime even smiled a bit. This one was new, a cautious smile.

"We helped her up, Dad, and showed her how Hydro could sit." Ryan pet the hound on the head, and the dog shifted and rolled over, colliding with Jaime's leg.

She jumped two inches into the air, making the boys collapse into giggles again.

"All right, comedians," Jaime said. "If you're gonna make fun, I'm leaving and taking my chocolate-covered peanuts with me. He doesn't scare me… exactly. He's just big!"

"He's a big baby." Ryan said and plopped down beside Hydro and laid across him, giving him a big hug. The dog just rolled on his back, enormous tongue lolling.

Tad laughed, charmed by the scene despite himself. "That's our Hydro… he's full of puppy love. Just a bit rambunctious."

"A bit? He was tenderizing my face."

"Hmmm… I'm almost jealous." He flashed his most charming grin. "Sorry about that, sugar." He shifted his attention to the boys, glad he'd amended his chore roster, if only to see Ryan coming out of his shell. Kid had been so quiet lately. "So, did you boys convince Miss Jaime to cook out with us?"

"Yeah," said Cal and a second behind his younger brother, Ry hollered, "Yeah! Yeah!" And the two boys hopped around, whooping like hyenas.

They wandered down to the river bank where a grill was smoking by a little picnic area. They made plates, no muss, no fuss, and throughout the munching of good grub, the boys vied for her attention, filling the air with their chatter and laughter.

"This is a balm for a lonely soul," Jaime said unexpectedly after dinner as she leaned back on the large green quilt Tad spread by the water to watch the boys and his oaf of a dog play.

Calvin and Ryan both had fruit jars with holes handily popped in by Tad's pocketknife. The kids were leaping for lightning bugs and the dog leaped around them, while seeming to keep them herded back from the water's edge. The boys weren't nabbing many of the little glow sticks flying about, but they were all having a blast.

She looped her arms behind her head and stretched out, crossing her legs tight at the ankle, eyes closed. The late day sun kissed her gently as it traveled closer to the end of its daily journey. With the sound of the river trickling nearby, and the kids playing and dog barking, he wondered what he was doing.

"You're not too shabby on the grill. If you cook like that in the kitchen, you might get recruited for all kinds of positions."

"Gee, what are you offering, Ms. Summers?"

With her eyes still closed, she must know he was watching her. There was a heat building, and he needed to snuff it out pretty quick. She was just here for the summer, and he had way too much to do to entertain a high maintenance girlfriend. Could he even consider dating? The love 'em and leave 'em kind of girl that apparently appealed to him would further damage the boys' opinions of women.

"Tomorrow, I start work for your sister. I'll be staffing several positions and..."

"Nah, I got something in mind. I don't want tugged into that touristy mess they got going on over there. So, are you considering this a date?"

"Nah. When a man takes a woman on a date, he asks her

nicely, not as if it were the neighborly thing to do. This is what neighborly folk do in rinkydink towns. I just came for the food, neighbor."

Leaning back on her elbows again, she grinned at the mock disappoint on his face. "This is a beautiful spot. Looks like we're going to have a stellar sunset. The way the sky is reflecting off the river takes my breath away. The pink, purple and orange tones would make a tie dye jealous."

"Yeah, I come out here all year long, hoping to catch a sunrise or sunset. The trout bite mercilessly there." He shaded his eyes against the riot of colors reflecting on the surface and pointed to a little boil of water upstream. "Underneath that little wave is a large rock and the fish just pop out of the water for you.

"So, what do you do, Tad, besides being a father and a good neighbor?" Jaime glanced at him curiously.

"What makes you think I don't work for the welcome wagon? What? That's a real thing around here. This might be a part of my job. Hydro, of course, is the official greeter…" He trailed off as she gave him a dry look.

"Handsome boys." Jaime raked her hand through her hair, gathering it into a ponytail, snapping on a glittery rubber band she'd worn on her wrist. "Where's their mom?"

Tad glanced at his boys, where the clumsy yellow hound was trying to wrestle a stick away from Ry. The two were making a great game of it while Cal practiced skipping stones.

"In St. Louis. She works for a law firm and made partner two years ago. Our divorce had been final for over a year. I'm in the final stages of getting full custody. Thankfully, Judith suggested a payout for the child support she'd be giving up and signed the papers. We have one more court date next month, and then we can all go our separate ways with no hard feelings. I want to bring my kids up here and instill a strong sense of responsibility."

He shrugged. "Honestly, I'm not too crazy about all that ruckus at my folk's old place, but it is what it is, and we all had to do what we had to do. I hope it doesn't spoil the neighborly values around here, though." He grinned, past ready to change the subject.

"No hard feelings, huh? You don't exactly strike me as that guy, but I'll buy it, sure. Here they come." Jaime sat up, tucking her legs underneath her, and he suspected she was ready to jump up and run if the dog got too close.

Cal and Ry ran up while Hydro trotted along and stopped short, laying down just beyond the blanket to watch Jaime curiously. Smart dog. The kids had stretched their shirts into baskets full of rocks and shells, which they dumped on the quilt at Jaime's knees.

"Look Dad, Miss Jaime." Both boys sat down, Ry watching Cal for pointers. "These are for our collections. Look at these."

"They're good, huh?" asked Ry, looking at Jaime.

Despite them being ordinary, she looked them over, and oohed and aahed appropriately. She even chose one from each boy when they offered. She had a knack with kids. He didn't think she'd appreciate hearing it.

Tad watched, and as he did, he knew he needed to think hard about this. He had no time. What effect would crushing on this fly-by-night girl have on his sons?

She was beautiful.

That was his only explanation for why he'd been sitting up here flirting with a woman and not down there skipping stones with his boys. The three of them were, well, reliant, and didn't need Jaime and her bad girl attitude in their life, not with all the irons he had balanced over the fire.

No sir, this would not be a casual friendship. This woman did something to him, and she knew it. Tad knew he liked it too much.

"Well, boys, time to get cleaned up for bed." He stood and began gathering the picnic supplies to take indoors.

"Ahh, do we have to go already?" Cal looked at him hopefully, and Jaime stood.

"Good call." Brushing off her cute derriere, she said, "I'm ready to hit the sack, too, guys. I'm bushed."

"All right, Dad. G'night Miss Jaime. C'mon Hydro." The

boys called out goodbyes and took off at high speeds toward the house while Jaime folded the blanket and laid it on his arm. "Thanks for this. I haven't been so relaxed in a while. It was nice of you, neighbor."

Tad grunted. His eyes lingered on her miniskirt and rhinestone slippers before he said, "If you're planning on staying here, sweetheart, you'd better get some more practical clothes."

With the little dig making him feel a little better, he retreated inside, leaving her to walk the short distance to his cabin in the dusk alone. He had to let go of the feeling of warmth that her sweet laughter brought him. Focus.

Chapter 3

One last glance in her visor mirror assured her she looked good. Every wild hair was tucked into a respectable braid, and she'd applied makeup from moisturizer to top coat, so her face would wear with the day.

At first light, Jaime had peeked out the window and seen Tad walking toward his garden. He got an early start, and she'd hit the hay way too late.

She'd successfully completed a late-night raid of a realm with her gaming buddies, and then snatched a few hours of restless sleep. Jaime was tired, but ready to rock. She didn't know what to expect today, but weekends would likely be hottest, so Tuesday was a good day to start. She'd be fine.

Her nerves wouldn't settle, though, until she met each employee, searching for the hidden gems she would find. People gave you their best work if you asked nicely and expected it. Some slandered her a headhunter, but she saw it as sifting the less desirable ingredients out, and repurposing them if she could.

People called her cold-hearted, but she was cool with that. Restaurant owners found satisfaction in well-run kitchens, and she left teams and kitchen families in her wake.

She stepped out of the VW's shelter into the moisture-laden air, bracing to suffer the humidity. She groaned as her feet touched the gravel, looking at her lucky flats. You'd think if

Wilcox was going to dump millions into a resort business, he'd blacktop. The boots and sneakers coming in her trunk couldn't get here fast enough. She tackled the steep gravel climb to the Clubhouse.

Halfway up the steep hill, breathless, she turned around, stalling. It was beautiful. The river itself snaked around the front of the large Mill overlooking the river, and the fog laid out wispy diminishing tails on either side of the building as the mists faded with the morning sun.

"Nice view."

Tad's sudden closeness left her hyper aware of him. His skin smelled like the river's edge, and the intoxicant filled her mind. His cool drawl sent shivers down her spine.

"The fishing is going to be good today, too."

Pulling herself together, she was wary of the flare of excitement that flittered in her at his nearness. "Why, Tad, what a pleasure. I thought you were playing in your garden this morning. Looking for damsels to disturb?"

Turning to face him, she wished she hadn't. The brooding cowboy had retreated and now looked ready for fun and adventure. Dark hair glinted with blond highlights in the morning sun, curling out from under his ball cap, and his camo eyes were sporting a playful glint. Her mouth watered at the wonderfully thick patch of brown chest hair curling from under his partially buttoned plaid shirt. The sloppy cargo shorts made him look like a kid, and lightweight vented sneakers and old school aviator shades in his pocket rocked the transformation.

"Wow, you look like you're here intending to have fun. No big chore list?"

"Promised the boys a fishing trip since they are out of school for the summer. Today's the day."

"I thought you didn't approve of what was going on down here?" Jaime asked with a nod at the semi-full resort sprawling around them.

"Well, this is the best takeout on the water, and I get a family discount. Seems a no-brainer. Besides, thought I might see you here." He looked around, then back at her. Grinned. "Maybe ask you for a date."

Jaime's heart was hammering. There was something different about Tad that had her humming, no lie. But she wasn't staying, and he had kids. People were liable to get hurt, and she didn't work that way.

"Look, you're real cute and all, but you're not my type." Jaime aimed herself back up the hill, careful not to slide and fall in to Tad. That would be just the ticket. If she fell on her butt again, he'd start calling her Grace. "No hard feelings, all right, neighbor?"

"Yeah, right." He slanted his eyes at her, considering. "I thought I caught a vibe. But sure, no hard feelings." His mustache curved over a lazy smile. "I've heard a lot about you, but nobody said you were so smart. Catch ya around, then. Neighbor."

He loped effortlessly down the hill she had just climbed, and she could hear the boys cheering from the farm truck below. Right before he got in, he turned around and gave her a lingering look, then hopped in and eased off to the landing. And she'd been staring after him.

Well, that sucked.

This would not blow her day. She chugged the rest of the way to the top of the hill and saw there was a parking lot on the far side of the building. Right. Pushing thoughts of everything else out of her mind, Jaime went about discovering the dragon that was hers to slay.

Shortages. Staff, food, supplies. The only things Lana and Garrett had going for them in ample supply were heart, money, and customers. She could work with that.

"Okay, so you guys are stretched, and money isn't fixing your problem. I was looking around yesterday, and I have some ideas. Let me play tourist today, form some impressions. I'll explore an empty cabin, grab a bite at the restaurant, have a drink downstairs, just get a feel for what you already have in place." Jaime leaned over the table where she, Lana, and Garrett had been putting all the cards down for the last hour and gave them a wry smile. "I'm probably going to change it all. I'm going to change restaurant hours, lengthen a few shifts, increase a few wages and responsibilities, trade people around. It can be uncomfortable, and if you guys don't want the works, I can just fill in for the summer until you get a handle on things."

"Please, Jaime," Garrett said. "Now that we know we're having a baby this fall," his deep voice held a vibration of panic, "there is no doubt in my mind I need several good managers. I can pay them if you can find them."

She nodded. "You got it. It will surprise you how many of the right people are already here. They just didn't understand the master plan. I expect by Labor Day, you two can watch this place run while you decorate the nursery."

"We don't expect any guarantees, and Garrett said he would gladly pay your fee—"

"Let me just do this, Lana, for old times' sake. I'll expect all expenses covered, and I'll charge two simple meals a day at the restaurant. I'll keep receipts. You already hooked me up with a place to stay. In exchange, I'll work on solutions for a minimum of 40 hours a week, for the next 90 days, and fill in as needed, restaurant or bar. Then we'll call this deal wrapped. You should be staffed and I'll be moving on. Sound good?"

Lana looked like she was going to argue about something, but Garrett didn't give her a chance. "Throw in drinks for you and any guests you might have on the house at the tavern for the summer, and a steak whenever you want it and you've got a deal. If you find me one or two good managers and a workable plan, we'll be forever grateful."

"All right then, we'll meet here in the morning. I'm off to play tourist."

"Thank you, Jaime. We're already grateful. There's a tour once a day, about ten that starts in front of the store here. You'll be just in time if you want to catch it. It's five bucks, so save your receipt." Her best friend smiled mischievously. "Oh, and tomorrow, if I were you, I'd drive around to the parking area. That steep hill can be a beast."

Jaime looked at Lana and laughed. She loved irony.

She fell in at the back of the tour. There was a family of five with kids, two older couples and a young couple, probably not married yet. Not bad for a Tuesday morning.

The tour guide was young, probably in her early twenties, but she had a wise look about her, and she seemed to know her job. Her long dark hair was plaited into double braids and topped off by a lovely red bonnet. She wore a matching pioneer dress with a white pinafore and reminded Jaime a lot of a young Laura Ingalls Wilder.

The tour was worth every penny.

Jaime and the group hiked a few short trails, got a cabin tour, took a brief look at the old cotton gin that was no longer in operation, then headed to the centerpiece of the tour. The remodeled mill inspired a sense of reverence. Her gaze roamed over the distinguished old building and she felt the low, reverberating hum of the machinery through her body.

She hadn't felt that yesterday. They must only turn on the machinery for the tours.

She had also come in from a side entrance yesterday, and that entry didn't command near the attention this one did. They painstakingly restored the three-story building and tweaked it with improvements.

A full wrap-around porch on two levels had an overlook deck on the top level that spoke of comfort and luxury. There were rocking chairs and benches grouped randomly, inviting diners to relax before and after their meals.

The front double doors opened into the building, and a bright light shone on a grain room encased in glass, immediately capturing the guest's attention. The tour went into the grain room and pulled the glass door shut behind them. The sound of the machinery was deafening. Their guide reached over and flipped a switch on the wall, quieting the machines. Her accent was fabulous and authentic, and the gentle lull of her story transported Jaime.

"A hundred years ago, this mill was the cornerstone of many families' food supplies for the year. Wagons full of corn, wheat, and oats would draw from as far away as Arkansas—" she paused dramatically, cueing the crowd to chuckle, since by car,

Arkansas was not so far, "and twice a year, people would pack their best clothes for visiting, and meet old friends outside this very door, to dance, drink, and celebrate their harvests, while endless lines of wagons backed up to the front of the building, and poured their hand-picked crops into the basement."

She gestured in a practiced movement. "Now, let's see how it works. Are you guys ready? I need a volunteer?" She chose the youngest of the group and told the guests they could cover their ears if they needed to. Then she flipped the switch to set the old stone buhr mill back into action. The young girl poured a basket of dried corn into a hopper and with the machines going, a big belt on the floor was being turned by the water wheel outside being spun by the millrace. Soon, beautiful white flour spewed out a funnel into a big cloth sack. "And that's how it works," their guide hollered. "Anyone else want to try?"

Jaime realized after her tour that she hadn't noticed how cool all this was when she was younger. This had just been a good place to hide from the parentals. Memories had been swamping her since she first turned into the parking lot. The three girls spent a lot of time down at the landing, tanning and boy watching, and they had been in their own world. BFF's.

They usually walked over from Lana's on weekends. Mr. and Mrs. Stone had always said it was like they had three daughters. Kat lived further down on Old River Road, but they always got to Lana's on the weekends. When Kat got her curves, Jaime's twin brother Jake added himself to the package. Then, they were a crew of four.

One night changed it all. If she had known what Kat and Jake were planning, she might have sabotaged the event. Instead, it had been all about her. And it cost her everything. But she wasn't into self-pity. Anymore.

She'd brought flowers for Lana's parents and took them to the graveyard on her way to town yesterday. It was something she had wanted to do for a while, and talking to their headstones had given her courage to come back.

She'd left devastation in her wake back then. It had taken a lot of work and some counseling, but Jaime knew she'd forgiven herself. But here, well, everyone knew her rambunctious teenage self. She guessed her rambunctious adult self wasn't liable to make a better impression.

Such as life.

After the tour, she wandered around outside the Mill room. The restaurant was to the left, with the kitchen and deck toward the right. There was a little gift shop outside the grain room where it looked like they had T-shirts, hats, and some locally made crafts, jellies, and breads.

She checked her cell and had a half an hour to spare before she planned to check out the restaurant. To best gage current operating standards, she would pick the optimum time for a lunch rush. Lana said it wasn't going great at the restaurant, but that was likely Lana being her sweet self.

Jaime went out on the deck and was glad to see another smoker, so she didn't need to ask. She wandered over to a neat feature of the deck, where it was built around a grand oak tree. She inhaled deeply on her vape, and exhaled a satisfying cloud, the sweet smell of caramel surrounding her.

He asked her on a date. Knowing who she was. Why? He had to see they were a non-starter. After spending half the night thinking about jumping him, she was pleased her will power won out.

He took it well. They'd be good.

After a bit, she wandered down a side staircase to the lower deck. Sweet set up. So, three dining rooms altogether. The restaurant was on the main floor, with its own small bar. The narrow top floor hosted parties, no kitchen, just a sink, so they must move the food up a flight of stairs manually for that. This lowest level was a posh screened-in deck with a full bar and a small kitchen.

Her brain was humming with ideas as she walked around…

There were two bandstands, one inside the screened area, and one outside where the deck just seemed to go on and on, promising live music and plenty of room for dancing.

The ambience was nautical. There was a canoe behind the bar to stock ice cold beer, a little fishnet hanging from the ceiling… It would do. Sounded like the issue was staffing and supply. Liquor probably wasn't presenting the same challenges as produce, but she needed to ask. She knew a guy…

All right, showtime. Jaime entered the restaurant through the front entrance and waited at the door to be seated, per the laminated note taped to the podium. From her position, she could see into the dining room and noted four tables of two and a table of three. She saw no staff moving around.

One couple was eating their meal, one couple had a bread basket, and the last two tables had drinks. It looked like the three-top had yet to receive any attention. Not necessarily terrible. Not great.

Laughter burst from the kitchen, followed by someone's cheerful swearing loud enough to fill the restaurant with lewd language. Why wasn't their music playing in the dining room? Kitchens were notoriously bawdy, so the music should always be on, in case the joking made it past the door. Soothes the savage beast and all…

Two scarred saloon doors swung open and out walked a gal with a tray, in assumably correct attire. She was cute, her short dark hair shading to purple underneath. The tattooed arm sleeves were a little much for Jaime's taste, but to each their own.

"Hey," she said as she cruised past Jaime into the dining room and dished out a lunch for one couple that didn't have bread. Swinging past the three anxious looking women, presumably to get a drink order, she stopped in front of Jaime again on her way back to the kitchen.

"Kinda busy today. Be awhile for I can get to ya." A silver tongue piercing flashed distractingly as she talked. "Still want me to seat ya?"

"Oh, please." Jaime pointed to the empty bar area next to the kitchen. "Could I get a seat in there?"

"I was trying to keep everybody together, but I guess. I'll be with ya soon." She disappeared into the kitchen and loudly resumed the conversation she was having with the cook.

Jaime couldn't help but smile. She was bartender material.

She meandered around the small lounge area, the view a perfect panorama of the rushing river below. The door from here led out to the deck where she'd visited with Lana yesterday. With a dubious glance at the kitchen her server disappeared into, Jaime explored.

On the deck, a couple from the morning tour was seated at the far end. They were clearly in the early stages of love, since they were still looking mushy despite fighting bees and flies off a nearly empty pitcher of margaritas.

From the lazy way the fellow moved, Jaime thought he had enjoyed the lion's share of that pitcher. This deck needed a screen too, maybe copper mesh so as not to obscure the view… a striped awning would be nice to offset the beer garden umbrellas below.

She walked to the edge of the porch railing, leaning on her elbows, studying the action on the river below. Returning canoes and kayaks dotted the takeout. When she was a teenager, she was afraid of floating over the five-foot manmade waterfall that spanned the river's breadth just below the takeout. What if you just couldn't stop?

Kat and Lana always made fun because she would get out of her tube or boat and try to walk the last bit of a float. With the millrace on one side and a waterfall that looked like a limb crusher spanning the ridge, she'd taken no chances.

The boats were colorful and varied, and so much more plentiful than they used to be. Fifty floaters in a couple of hours where you used to might see ten all day. From her vantage point on the deck, it was like looking down on a carnival from a plane. The boats mostly shuttled calm looking middle-aged folks who had enjoyed their morning. In her experience, the less sober customers would be in full force on Saturdays.

She was about to turn away, wondering if her server had noticed her absence yet, when a glimmer of movement in the dappled shadows at the far end of the waterfall caught her eye. Four little arms and two fishing poles were waving at her.

She grinned, falling a little more in love with the two little golden boys. She threw her arms up in a double wave and laughed as they fell against each other, splashing in the water. The dog was watching the action calmly from the bank, and Tad stood in the shadows. Whether or not they fooled around, the man was eye candy. But no wave from him. If he was smiling at the boys' outrageous splashing, she couldn't tell.

Were they good?

The second she stepped out onto the porch, he moved out of the sunshine and into the darkness, his mind a storm of murky emotions. Trouble. He'd known. Her moves oozed sensuality that had a man wondering what it might be like to have her for his own.

Was he willing to trade sanity for a chance to run fingers through her wild mane of hair, now so neatly pinned into a braid... a moment to stare into her coy eyes and see that "come and eat me up" look? Would the taste of those full lips that so easily twisted into a sly smile or a perfect pout drive him over the edge?

Just do it and be done with it. He laughed at himself. Yeah, right. Sounded like an addiction in the making, and he was ready to sign up, despite all the rational work he'd put in to solving the problem throughout the night.

But she turned him down.

That was good. Tad would get on with the summer challenge of building a home for his boys. If he could just quit thinking about her long legs, and wondering and wishing.

"Dad, can you get her for us? She's pretty, and we like her." Tad looked down at his youngest son and ruffled Ry's hair. He suspected Cal put Ry up to asking since he was craning his ear for the answer. Then he looked at Ry carefully and realized he didn't know which of them might be most smitten.

"Sorry, buddy. That girl is way out of our league. And I'm an old guy who likes things just the way they are." Tad took a deep breath. Way too old to learn how to date again. Things were a lot different, and he had no desire or time to learn. He was good.

"But she likes you, Dad. She smiled at you a bunch last night.

And she played with us. How come you didn't smile at her? We like her. Cal says you can get her for us."

"He does, huh?" Tad glanced at his firstborn, and asked himself why life was so complicated for his kids. He'd had a relatively normal childhood. Why hadn't he been able to provide that for them?

"Listen guys, I know it's been a tough year, and me and your mom haven't made it easy for you. We have a new house, and you'll be starting a new school... we'll have a different life because your mom isn't here."

"She was never home anyway," Calvin said.

"I know that hasn't been easy for you. You guys are too young to understand yet, but your mom loves you. She just has a hard job and..."

Calvin interrupted him. "Don't BS us, Dad. We're kids, but we ain't dumb."

Tad took another deep breath. Did he prefer questions he had no answers to?

He herded the boys over to the bank and told them to prop up their poles and grab sodas from the cooler. Ryan brought him one, too. They sat with their feet in the water, and both boys slurped their sodas, then started sifting and throwing river rocks into the water.

Thank God for the river. Whenever Tad was feeling spun out, just a few minutes to pitch a few rocks at the river always helped him gear up for the next play. Helped his mind. He grabbed a few rocks and chucked them.

"So, here's the deal, guys, and it is what it is. We're bachelors now and we need to stick together. The chores your mom used to pay someone to do—we get to do them. I got Hydro, but any other critters you get, you gotta take care of them, 100%."

"We can have pets?" Calvin asked. "What if I want a snake?"

"Eww..." Ryan shook his head. "Yuck."

"Maybe a lizard," Tad said. "But no getting off track here. We are sitting here talking instead of catching that monster crawdad over there because we need to get some things lined out about women. By the way Cal, we'll talk about language choices later. But as you pointed out, you are kids, and intelligent ones. I hope so, because we got a tough road ahead. Us guys must survive the summer with no maids and no moms."

"After summer, can we get one of each?" Ryan asked, looking hopeful.

"No." Tad tried not to sigh aloud this time. "After summer, we'll be doing the same stuff, but you'll be starting school here, so we'll figure that out then."

The environment at the kids' school near St. Louis was toxic, and the trouble at home was creating attitude problems. He'd been adamant the boy's come out of that school system. He hoped the small local school wouldn't put them at a disadvantage for activities, but for now, they had summer ball lined up, and heaven help him, he'd signed up to coach.

"What if we need a maid?" Calvin asked.

"We don't. We'll have chore lists. Back to women. My job as a dad is to make sure you boys know how to take care of yourselves and behave like gentlemen when necessary. That way, when you grow up and meet the right woman, she won't toss you out on your ear because you don't know how to cook or clean up after yourself. It's a possibility. Trust me."

"What if we meet the woman of our dreams but we're too young or too old for her?" Ryan wanted to know.

Could the ground just open and swallow him? "Uhm, well, I guess that's life's hard knocks. You roll with it and try to be ready when the next chance happens."

"Are you sure you're not just being chicken, Dad?" Cal asked.

"All right, Mr. Mouth. What's in your craw?"

"Nothing." Cal stood up with a skipping stone and winged it, getting three jumps.

Tad felt a swell of pride. They'd only been working on that for a week.

"It's just, we heard you telling all those old ladies that we were fine and we didn't need no woman, but are you sure? That we don't need a mom?"

Crushed. "Guys, I can't make any promises one way or another on that. I can tell you, if I make some decisions about a girl, any girl, I'm going to make those decisions first, as the dad. If a girl is nice enough, and I want you guys to meet her, I might bring her around, but that does not mean she will be your mom. Your Mom will always be that, and even though she's may not know how to show you guys love, don't let that stop you from loving her back, okay?"

Someday your mama might be gone when you need her the most. If he brought a woman into their lives, it needed to be someone soft who would tell them bedtime stories and sew them Halloween costumes and bake cookies. Like his mama had.

"I guesses," rolled out of his minions and he assumed that was the best he was going to get.

"One more thing. If ever the time comes, if ever I were to consider getting married again, it would be a family decision. I'm still the boss, but I care what you guys think. We're a team."

The boys grinned at him and all three put their hands in the air and wiggled their fingers, hollering at the top of their lungs, "Go, Team!"

Chapter 4

Jaime pushed open the vintage screen door at the Clubhouse, shaking off her jitters. With a friendly wave, she slipped past the young couple standing at the check-in desk, a scarred wooden beast they called a workstation. The couple was cute, and so was the dark-haired girl working behind the beast. She was managing the couple's paperwork and two phone calls near simultaneously. She gave Jaime a brief nod as she passed to the back offices. Jaime ran into Lana in the hall.

"Do I need to ask Garrett to haul you to your house and sit on you until you get some rest?" Jaime asked. "You look beat. Do you feel okay?"

Lana brightened up, but there was a tiredness in her face that shouldn't be there this early in the morning.

"Tuckered out. If you dare tell Garrett you think I look tired, you will bear the brunt of my wrath." Lana tugged on Jaime's braid to soften the probably very real threat. "The man is wearing me doing with his worry for the baby. I wish he would just go back to worrying about the resort and leave all the baby stuff to Mother Nature."

Lana pulled her rubber band out of her wheat hair, and pulled her hair back again, reclaiming the escaped strands.

"He's in the war room, c'mon." She pushed the door open and motioned to Jaime's chair from the day before. Garrett was chilling at the round table, eating a cookie from the platter in the center. That would be Lana's touch.

"So," Garrett said. "Turn our lives upside down so you can fix our glitches, fixer."

Jaime sat down and pushed her tablet out in front of her. She wouldn't need it, but just in case.

"I recommend three managers that all report to one of you. A campground manager, a bar manager, and a restaurant manager. Right now, you two are shifting a little of everything back and forth between you. Do you want to keep sharing dual responsibilities or…"

"Campground," Lana said.

"Restaurant," Garrett said.

They grinned at each other.

"I was thinking about the restaurant, Jaime," Garrett said. "Since you opted to take over the scheduling for the summer— I still think you're crazy, but I'm thrilled—these operating hours you propose… It gives me courage to indulge in an idea."

He took a deep breath. "Let's give me the restaurant hours. I planned to cook when I started this, but things just didn't play out that way. So far, I have seen zero time inside the kitchen. I'll keep driving the boat bus in the mornings. If you schedule me a couple of boat flippers to manage the boats at the put-in and the takeout, I should be able to handle the 12-hour days on the weekends. It kind of sounds like a break." He finished with a laugh.

"Done. What are you doing with Laura Ingalls Wilder when she isn't giving tours?" Jaime asked.

"Mel? She cleans cabins on the weekends. That tour was her idea, and the outfit was her great grandma's. She's local, lives over the river a short piece."

"How do you feel about her as your right hand here in the Clubhouse? She fielded every touristy question I threw at her. She's a gem."

"Yeah…" Lana breathed. "And do I get to keep Jane? She was at the front desk when you came in."

"Do you think we could get her to work mornings shifts at the store in the, and hostess at the restaurant on Friday and

Saturday evenings?"

"I can ask if she'd be game," Lana said. "And I can cover those days."

Jaime shook her head. "I am hoping we can use Mel to help take the pressure off there. We'll have to find another housekeeper…"

"Two more. One of my girls quit last Friday. Moving to Memphis to sing." Lana shrugged. "I told you it was bad."

"Okay." Jaime frowned. Two housekeepers. "I'm liberating your waitress to serve downstairs. She looks like she can handle herself with the butt pinchers."

"We haven't been able to keep a waitress down there." Garrett said. "I have a good bartender, but she's not reliable, and I've been drafting the boat boys who are old enough to haul alcohol for her. I'm afraid she's going to quit if we don't get her some help."

"She'll have it." She flipped open her computer to look over her graph of housekeeping duties and made some notes. "We're going to find at least two more steady bartenders who will multitask. I expect them to mix, sling beer, throw a pizza in the oven or fix a plate of nachos when needed to compensate for the hours we shut down the restaurant throughout the week. We'll have to pay them accordingly."

Garrett nodded and Jaime made a few more entries in her tablet.

"By my calculations," Jaime said, "that will up the desirability of the upstairs dining experience, and we can time the grocery deliveries so all the ingredients will always be fresh. That should eliminate this out-of-control waste list you have."

"Well," Garrett said with a scowl, "part of that was my glorious chef calling it waste and carting it off. I let him go, but we're still facing the issue of availability."

"Good to know. How 'not reliable' is your bartender?" Jaime asked.

"Well, we suspect she knew the chef was stealing from us and didn't mention it. She's always here on the weekends when the money is good, but not so much during the week. Her kids are sick a lot, so I don't know."

"Right on. We'll just find her some additional incentive to keep those kiddos well." Jaime tugged on her braid, thinking. "What about the line cook working with purple hair chick over there? Do you trust him?"

"Yeah, he's a good kid," Garrett said. "Got some family problems, but hopefully he can overcome them. He's a quick learner. I had our chef training him. I'm not sure if he knew about the thefts, but I don't believe he had a part in it."

"I'll get you a prep cook and a line cook, too, and we'll keep your dishwasher. He's a sweet kid. Are you comfortable making this guy your second in command? What was his name?"

"Zack. Yeah, I think if I could work with him for a while, he'd get what I want to do. He could help when we have the baby, and after, if I'm lucky." Garrett nodded and stood. "I'm a lot more excited about this summer. If there is anything else I can do, speak up, whenever. I'm thankful that you've taken some of the load off, but I still want to stay in the loop."

"I should be good, and we'll make sure all loops circle back to you," Jaime reassured him. "I'll fill the slot at the bar until we find you a manager and get them trained. I figure if you keep the bar and grill open noon to eight during the week, that should catch any of the restaurant traffic we might miss. We'll have to keep Mel free to do at least one tour a day, but I'll try not to overwork her. She can direct people downstairs rather than to the restaurant. If we create a practical sandwich menu, we should be able to handle those shifts with a versatile bartender and our waitress. What's her name, with the purple hair?"

"Staci," Lana supplied.

"Yes, let's see if Staci is good with her new job. Maybe she'll be interested in mixology. I'll take the weekend shifts with your bartender until I can get a few more hired and trained. Scheduling and interviewing I can do wherever in the mornings, and I'll monitor how it goes down there during the week. I'll be full in on the weekends."

Ouch, that was going to cut in to her gaming time.

Lana and Garrett looked at each other. "This is more than

we expected," Garrett said.

"We have our missions, crew. I will communicate with your people that they are training for a well-paid, year-round, long-term position if they want it, and I'm counting on ya'll to back that up. I think you got this. I reckon we're set to roll the dice."

Lana hopped up, pushing a wooden chair she'd been sitting on under the table. "You are a force to be reckoned with, Miss Summers," Lana teased. "Glad to have you leading our crew!"

Jaime gave them both her most reassuring smile. "I'm going to grab a smoke. Meet ya'll back here in thirty for team intros."

The dreaded introductions. "Hi, I'm your new boss. You're demoted if not fired, and I'm not staying." Everyone loved that.

To her surprise, the intro meeting went well, with only one major disappointment. The bartender got married over the weekend to a biker from up North, and she'd only stopped by to let them know she and her kids were on their way out of town.

Lana would help her tonight to get the feel of things, since she had worked behind the bar several times.

Jaime heard Lana on her way back to the little office in the Clubhouse. There wasn't much real estate here to spread out, so Jaime had been considering heading up the hill to her cabin and roughing out a little office.

"Crying over the schedules yet?" Lana asked as she breezed into the room. "I know when Garrett is working on schedules cause he's cranky a full day before and a full day after."

She walked over to a fridge and grabbed a bottled water, then set it down without opening it to pick up a box of new t-shirts. She started folding as she talked. "I'm so excited Garrett spoke up about cooking. He's excited, I can tell."

"Since I was worried about filling spots with ourselves as laborers, which rarely lasts long, I'm thrilled Garrett wanted to be in the kitchen. I didn't expect that."

Lana chuckled. "Oh, I did. He's a wonderful cook, he just hasn't had time to focus on it since he's been making sure all the cabins were up to par on plumbing and heat and air for the year. We've had two not fun plumbing surprises already." She fanned herself. "I just can't believe that our chef was stealing. He had been Garrett's good friend back in culinary school, and he had seemed like a good fit. It was an expensive mistake."

"At least you caught it quick. I think the damage should be reparable. The menu redesign we worked on this morning will cater to patrons on different levels, from the campground locals to the tourists to destination diners. His menu was fraught with waste, which made it easier for him to scam you."

Lana nodded thoughtfully, and Jaime continued.

"That leaves me bartending, which sounds fun since I usually end up in the kitchen, but it's liable to add fuel to the fire for the gossips."

"Jaime, what's really on your mind? I hear what you're saying, all useful, but it's not why you're here, is it?"

"It's Tad and Lug. Are they both against us? Why would your brother do that? I can understand Dad just being ticked off at me, but Tad… what's his deal?"

Lana sighed. "Some people just don't like change. Being one of those people myself, I know. Can you blame him? Tad came home looking for things to be the way they were so he could raise his kids with old school values. When he gets here, he convinces me to be open to opportunity, and I shack up with opportunity, thus converting the simple life around here into an exciting moneymaker. The town wasn't exactly for Garrett's lofty ideas, but we've converted mostly everyone, one by one."

She grinned. "I've got a plan to win your dad over. Tad, not so much. He sees this as corruption, in a way. Tourists tramping all over his river. We did kind of feel like it was ours when we were kids. He just takes longer to accept things."

"He's a real pain. What kind of man is content to stand around with cows all day?"

"My brother, and incidentally, your dad. Have you been to your old place?"

It was Jaime's turn to sigh. "The invitation hasn't exactly been forthcoming… you're not saying my dad bought cattle?"

"I am. Just about a dozen head, but he bought them a few years after your mom left. Just started drinking and pushing cows around. I think that was how he dealt with everything coming apart. He replaced his family with cows that don't talk back." Lana sat back with a cheeky smile. "Makes sense after all the trouble you and Jake gave your mama through."

"Speaking of my mama, I got a message from her this morning. Seems she got wind I was in the neighborhood, and that you have a cabin available for her to come for a visit. You have a cabin for my mama and not for me?"

"Sure, as soon I got a cancellation on cabin 2 for the Fourth of July weekend, I called your Mom and invited her to see you in action. Wasn't that sweet of me?"

"Lana! As if there wasn't enough upheaval in your life, you're going to turn this place into a battleground for senior citizens on the rampage?"

"I highly doubt your folks are rampaging. They've been separated long enough; I doubt they are going to be difficult."

"Hmph." Jaime shook her head. "Obviously, you don't remember my mom. Do you have any idea how long she can nurse a grudge?"

"Well, sweetie, if you're any sign, I'd say a heck of a long time. Don't you think it's about time your family gives up some grudges? I told you I had a plan to win over your dad. Surely you inferred I planned to meddle?"

At Jaime's glare, Lana softened her voice. "Jaime, really. You're at war with Kat and Jake, who, in your non-meddling absence, allowed their marriage to deteriorate. I think if you all start forgiving yourselves, it would heal some of the hurt that torments your family."

Jaime planned to say something rude. Instead, she gave up, dropping her head to her hands. Lana was quiet, letting her sulk.

"So now that you're pregnant, our roles are reversed and you're the one with all the advice?" She looked up at her friend. "So how does one go about convincing everyone she's forgiven herself for indirectly causing the death of the parents of her best friend and not come off like a total jerk? I don't know how to act."

Lana stood and came around the desk, leaning on an oak

chair stacked high with books.

"You start by admitting it wasn't even indirectly your fault. We were all three capable of making our own decisions at seventeen, and we just got caught doing what we'd been doing for a year already. Because Sheriff Tate arrested us instead of giving us a warning, is it his fault my parents were on the road? No one can say what could have happened differently, and I don't see any point in trying. My folks are gone, but they lived good lives. Tad and I are good people because they raised us to be good people, even when they weren't here. I wish they could meet their grandchildren, but Jaime, it was an accident."

"But…"

"No buts. And if you say it was your fault for bringing the weed, I'll beg you to remember I scored the wine, and the whole idea was Kat's plan to get Jake to marry her."

Jaime scowled. "She tricked him…"

"Whatever. I think you need to get over yourself here." Lana began pacing around the table, effectively dodging stacks of books without seeming to notice them.

"Your twin was in love with Kat, and you know as well as I do, they had the real thing. Jake was leaving, though. Wanderlust had him bad before you guys even moved here. Maybe he might not have left so abruptly, but that was Lug's hardheadedness, much as anything. Kids elope, people die, life goes on. I just wish… anyway. You need to get your act together."

"What do you think I've been doing for the past ten years? I'm successful…"

"Running. I think you have figured how to run from anything permanent, and you're successful at it. Don't look at me like that. You've been lecturing me for years, so you need to suck it up. I thought about challenging you to stay here for more than the summer—for at least a year. Bet you couldn't do it."

"That's crap. I don't run from anything," Jaime said. She wouldn't accept the challenge, though. It was not a gamble she could make confidently.

She looked up from pushing at her cuticles when she heard a thud. She jumped up, and with growing concern, leaped over a chair to where Lana had collapsed. One second, she'd been standing there fanning herself, the next moment, Lana was lying on the wooden floor. She regained awareness a second later.

"Just got too hot." Lana's breathing was shallow, and she was red as a cardinal. "I was going to sit, but I didn't make it."

"Geez, you scared the life out of me." Jaime helped Lana up and to a low chair, where Lana collapsed. Hurrying to the sink, she wet a cloth, and brought it back to press against Lana's forehead. "Should I call the doctor?"

"Just Garrett, please. He'll be hysterical for a minute, but I might need the afternoon off." She tried a smile. "Who would have thought I'd get all delicate? This little one better not be planning to be a wimp. I don't plan to lie around for the next six months."

Jaime flipped out her cell and called Garrett. He was on his way, so she grabbed another cold cloth for the back of Lana's neck.

Garrett came running in, frantic. He cradled Lana gently in his arms before pulling back to examine her. "Baby, are you okay? Did you hit your head? Where does it hurt?"

"I'm okay. I didn't hit my head, just banged up my pride. Right now, I feel embarrassed and hot. Can you take me home? I'm going to sleep it off." She turned to Jaime. "Don't worry, okay. I promise I'm fine."

"Garrett, you'll stay with her, right?" Jaime couldn't help worrying, no matter how tough her friend was.

"I won't leave her side until she makes me." His determination made Lana smile, though she rolled her eyes.

"Thanks, Jaime. Sorry I won't be around to help with the party of fishermen tonight. I think they'll be low key, hopefully," Lana said, her forehead furrowing.

"Don't sweat it. You rest. I've got this covered." Jaime's cavalier attitude faded when Garrett ushered Lana to his rig.

This was not going according to plan.

Jaime let a tired groan slip out. It had been a long time since she'd actually worked the floor, and as she rubbed the tired spots on her back, which seemed to be... well, her whole back, she remembered why she loved this job. With a grin, she tapped her pocket, which was stuffed with a wad of cash. The fisherman had been fun and generous, however long-winded.

She was walking toward her car when she noticed a truck sitting across the parking lot with its running lights on. Her heart picked up a few paces. It was never a good sign when there was a customer still waiting outside a full hour after the bar closed. Either she had her a drunk customer, or a stalker, either way she didn't have the patience for it.

It didn't seem she was going to have a choice, though. She watched out of the corner of her eye as she unlocked her car. As she opened the door, a cowboy boot thudded against the ground, and the parking lot lamp illuminated Tad's silhouette.

"I didn't want you to worry that I was a stalker. Lana said you worked alone, so I came to make sure you get back to the ranch safely."

His voice was warm and mellow, and Jaime wished she could walk over and climb in with him. If that wasn't the sweetest...

"If you insist on continuing to make such foolish decisions, you might need to find a keeper."

"Thanks, Ace, but I can take care of myself."

She thought he'd argue. He seemed to do that, but he just cleared his throat gruffly and climbed back into his truck. He followed her the short distance to the ranch and was inside his place before she even got out of her car.

She would have liked someone to visit with while she unwound a little, but apparently, she'd offended him with her lack of need for a chaperone. Well... his concern. Geez, did she have to be so nasty? He was just being nice... Or was he? He seemed pretty judgey. She shook her head at her own insecurity and let herself into the dark cabin.

Chapter 5

Tad was still restless as the hour of midnight approached. He held his breath and checked that his kids were sound asleep, pocketed a cigar from a box in his office, and stepped out onto his recently built porch to breathe in the early summer night air.

He looked at the cabin across the yard he had helped his dad build when he was a teenager. He'd lived in it his first three months back, before the house and kids arrived. His house was new, prefab, but it was nice. Rustic. He'd started building this porch immediately, the porch he and his dad had talked about building on the cabin someday.

Thinking about the cabin's history was more calming to him than entertaining his inappropriate thoughts about the woman with the disputable reputation who was inside.

She was a temptation. He briefly indulged his imagination with the stunning body of Jasmine Summers. The light went out in her cabin, and he imagined her sliding between his sheets. He'd seen her step out earlier in a little robe and doubted she wore anything under.

He'd never sleep in that cabin again without thinking of her. Honestly, he wondered if he could lie in any bed and not think of her. Risky notions. He took the cigar out of his pocket, debated lighting it. Put it back in his pocket.

He meant to go in, but he just sat in the dark, the cool air on his skin, listening to the river's song. After a while, he saw the nymph he'd been fancying step out of her cabin wearing the little white robe. It was too far to make out her features, but she seemed to float across the lawn down to the river bank, then sank to the grass.

It put him to mind of a scary movie where a seductive vampiress haunts the night.

The boys were crashed, and he'd left Hydro to guard the house… he grunted and got off the porch swing to go check on her. He padded through the grass on bare feet. There was a light dew in the grass, so it surprised him she sat down without stretching out something to sit on.

He was just about to announce himself when he heard her crying. He hadn't heard her over the river's murmur, but he was close enough now. The deep sobs seemed to bubble over. He hesitated.

Whatever had her upset was her business, and he thought it would embarrass her to be seen as vulnerable. He should just slip away.

"Hey, darling, looks like you could use a friend."

She said nothing for a long moment, then her reedy voice broke the quiet. "Why would you want to be my friend?"

She sounded unsure of herself, which, in the brief time he'd known her, was totally out of character.

Cautiously, he sat down on the bank a couple of feet from her. Like a friend would, not like a douchebag crushing on a crying girl. "Why wouldn't I?"

She rubbed the heels of her hands under her eyes a couple times, wiping away tears, then sniffed loud in the night. An owl hooted.

"I don't know. I never fit in here before, and ya'll are rigid, so it's not likely I'll fit in any better now. I don't think I should have come back. That's not all, really. I know you know who I am. I have no secrets here, and probably most everything you've heard about me is true. I'm no angel."

She glanced at him so he put on an understanding face, but he was having a tough time not laughing. She was bawling because she thought no one wanted to be her friend? All the guys were certainly vying for the chance.

"I didn't accuse you of being an angel. I didn't even come home for my parents' funeral, so I'm no hero."

"I wondered about that. Why didn't you? Not being judgmental here, but Lana looked up to you more than anything. She was always talking about you. If your mom wasn't the same way, I would have thought you were just another of her imaginary friends. She could have used her big brother."

Tad let out a deep sigh. "I know. That was a tough time. Judith was having false labors with Cal and I couldn't leave her. Lana said she was all right, and I needed to believe her. My ex and I were having problems before she found out she was pregnant, and well, then… we tried to make it work. It was important to both of us then. Her priorities changed as her career soared and we became an inconvenience to her."

He shared the facts of his life like a laundry list, determined not to share how painful this time in his life had actually been, but hopefully tell enough to help her relax so she could get whatever was really bugging her off her chest.

"She nearly aborted Ry, but we worked through his birth with counseling. When she asked for a divorce, I was relieved, though I hated to quit on the boys. Being an awesome dad to them was my primary mission."

"You don't have to tell me all this if you don't want." Jaime slid closer to him, presumably for body warmth. He was certainly generating plenty since he was hyper-aware of her.

"It's okay. Their Mom will probably be around at some point this summer, hopefully to visit them. Since it seems like we're going to be friendly neighbors, I thought you should know where things stood between us."

"Where do things stand between us?" Jaime asked him. "I thought we were pretty clear there was no 'us,' but here you are at midnight on the banks of the Falls with the likes of me. What exactly are we doing or not doing here?"

"I know you passed the boy's vetting process hands down but…" Even though he tried to make his voice sound playful, he meant what he was saying. "I haven't finished working you over yet. So, you were telling me what happened to you when you left Riverbend Falls? I heard you went to San Francisco."

"Hold your horses, cowboy. Just because you shared your sob story doesn't mean I'm spilling mine."

She poked him in the ribs and he grinned. He thought he was humoring her. "C'mon, spill."

She smiled back. Moonlight shadowed her features, but she was so appealing.

"All right, short and sweet. I went to San Francisco. Despite Lugs plans for mine and Jake's educations, we both went our own ways. I convinced my mom to sign me into the Treasure Island Job Corps, and I studied Culinary Arts. It was cool, and I tried to learn every aspect from the front to the back of a restaurant. I always enjoyed tinkering around the kitchen, but I didn't know if that was what I really wanted to do. Cooking is a hobby for me, and if you do it as a job, is it still a hobby?"

She stretched her legs out in front of her, kicking up dew droplets like rain. She cracked her ankles and pulled her legs back under her. How did all that leg curl up so tight?

"Anyway, one instructor gave us a short course on bartending, just basics really, and I fell in love. I looked it up online, studied the requirements, downloaded and memorized recipes… While the rest of my graduating class fought over the twelve culinary positions available, I was already shipping my resume around. Slightly inflated, but you know how that goes, and I had three jobs in three towns. I'd always wanted to travel, so my idea was born. I branded myself a fixer, and here I am, ten years later and a lot richer."

"How much have you traveled?"

"I've been in twenty-two cities for at least three months. It was awesome at first… The city never sleeps. We moved here when I was fourteen and it devastated me! Most of my childhood we'd lived near army bases or on base, and the quiet here was enough to drive me buggy. If I hadn't met Lana and Kat, I would've run away or something crazy like that."

He chuckled. "You really are a troublemaker, aren't you?"

"I'm owning it."

"So, you said it used to be awesome, but to hear you talk, you can't wait to be off on your next job. Do you ever want to slow down? Just stay in one place?"

"I mean, it hasn't happened yet." She shrugged. "Look, I've got something I want to ask you about, if you're sure we're friends?"

Here came the actual stuff. Whatever had her crying.

"I want you to work with me at the bar on the weekends until I can get a few more bartenders hired. Then you won't have to stalk me from afar."

The sneaky little minx. Was this whole setup a ruse? "No way. Did Lana put you up to this?"

"Up to what?" Jasmine asked innocently.

"I told you I'm not interested in working for them. I have my own ideas."

"To run yourself in the ground building a cattle herd so you can earn enough money to take people fishing?" Jaime unfolded that lovely leg and gave his bare foot a nudge with her toe. "Look, I'm not saying you don't get to do what you want. I'm just saying maybe you be a part of this thing your sister's building, instead of against her."

Tad shook his head, but Jaime went on.

"You know, we could make a deal…"

He turned away. This was a rabbit-hole.

"Wait, Tad, you want to help your sister out, right?"

"Not especially," Tad mumbled, pulling out his cigar, biting the end off and spitting it. Firing it up, ahhh.

"C'mon, sure you do. Think long term. You're wanting to run several hundred head of cattle on this land, and you're planning for it to be as much of a growing concern as your sister hopes her resort will be. She needs help right now because we are going to have a grand opening season. I believe we… she can keep this baby going and that will enable people to live and work year round, which will provide more residents making the job pool bigger, creating ranch hands you need."

He turned back, considering. That part sounded good.

"What are you proposing, exactly, if I was hypothetically interested?"

"We trade services," Jaime said, sending out sparks of her enthusiasm. "I can give you a hand on weekday mornings, any job you need done around here. I may not know how to do everything, but I learn quick. Friday and Saturday night, you're mine."

Oh, he wished.

"Behind the bar, you use that charm and familiarity to help me catch the locals, all ages. They love you. I need you."

"A bartender? How is that going to look?" Tad shook his head. "No, I don't think so."

"It's going to look like you accept what your sister is trying to accomplish, and that you're encouraging others to do the same. Honest, babe, you're perfect for it. It's an honorable gig with benefits. Tips are awesome. You can spend the extra ready cash on the boys or offset the costs of the ranch. It's just for the summer. I'll actively be trying to fill the positions, so I'm not exactly sure how long."

"I'm no bartender, but I know how to mix a few drinks." He leaned back in the wet grass, allowing himself to appreciate her closeness and not try to figure out if she was, in fact, naked under that little scrap of silk.

"See? Win-win. I'll help you out, you help me out. By the end of the summer, you should be able to have a ranch hand in place, so you can fish, and your sister will be well on her way. We'll do a little teamwork."

It sounded plausible and fun. Irresponsible. He looked at her and wanted very much to spend the summer with her.

"That seems like an awful lot of togetherness. The tantrums you indulge in? That's not how ranch hands act. I know you know your stuff, so I'm sure you can cover my butt behind the bar, but why would you want to?"

"You'll be great, Tad. You are eye candy, and we'll look good together behind the bar. I need some muscle to back me in crowds. You can sling beer for me, and I'll mix for us, unless you want to give it a shot. You need me and your sister needs you. I can help you if you help her."

"What about the boys? I don't have a sitter. I haven't needed one…" He was hooked.

"We could find someone to come and stay with the boys for you on the weekends."

He was getting in over his head in a hurry, but he didn't want to back out now.

"When would you start?" Tad stood up, and she rose to stand beside him. Had he realized what a perfect height she was for him?

"I could start in the morning. You start Friday? Six to midnight? Last call's at eleven."

"I'll talk it over with Cal and Ry, see if they're okay with the idea. Then we'll negotiate terms for a trial period, okay?"

"How very awesome of you, Dad."

She moved closer to him, and he watched her, a smoky heat igniting in her eyes. She slid her hands up his chest softly, leaning her body in behind her hands to mold to him. It was a nice fit. She was a nice fit. She moved her lips close to his.

"Will we be indulging in any extracurricular activities? Because I can't stop thinking about kissing you."

He touched his lips to hers, watching her intently, and felt urgent desire. Her eyes drifted closed as the kiss deepened, and she was weightless in his arms. The kiss lingered as he tasted her, and he wanted to lay her back down and indulge in all her lovely soft places. Tad felt her hair silkily dragging across his cheek, caught by the coarse hairs of his whiskers as they grew out from having grown a day too long. He groaned inwardly. He wanted her, bad.

"I want to take a chance on you, Jasmine Summers."

She pulled away, leaving him holding air where he'd been so eager for flesh.

"Hold on. There won't be any taking chances on me. We indulge in a little harmless sex, and when it's over, we're done. No chances to be taken."

"Nope. If you want in, you're all in. I'm not setting myself up to put my boys through heartbreak." Let alone him. What did she think he was, a sadist?

Jaime stepped away from him, cold slipping in where she'd stood. She stared at the half-moon as it mirrored its image on the water.

She seemed so controlled. Tad wondered how he felt he knew her at all. What was he doing out here?

If only she would check her arrogance. Maybe they could create a way for her to fit in. "What would it take to get you to stop blaming yourself, Jaime? You try to take the world's worries on your own shoulders…"

He moved behind her, tentatively laying his hands on her shoulders. Nothing scared him more than physical contact with this woman, and he could think of nothing he wanted more. Very physical.

"When are you going to face facts? You can't fix everything, no matter how hard you try. I've watched you with my sister and my kids. You've a nurturing nature, but I think you don't see it. You're used to guarding your heart with barbed wire."

"I think you're reading more in to me than there is." She spoke so softly he barely heard her.

"Sweetheart, I think you're cutting the line before you even see if you have a fish. I think you're a keeper worth fighting for."

"Scratch that." She pulled away again, and he was determined to keep his hands off her this time. Time was what she needed, and he had plenty of it.

If only things weren't so complicated with his ex…

"Look, let's get some sleep and wake up friends. I'll talk to the kids. We'll see. I want to help my sister."

"Deal," she said. "Now why don't you take off before we cross boundaries we regret."

Her tone wasn't angry, not really even disappointed. She had only been thinking about sex. Not like he had any more noble motivation, but he wouldn't sell out for it. He left her at the riverbank and trudged up to his house. With a simple command to go check it out, he sent Hydro out to watch her. Then he checked on the boys. Still sleeping. He went to his own bed and tried not to think of her until the sun came up.

The dog slipped up beside her and quietly laid his chin on his front paws as he crouched a few feet from her. She hoped Tad hadn't come back. She had foregone logging on and went down to the water to clear her mind. She had no inkling of how the crying fit had begun and was ashamed he'd caught her.

At least it had cleared the air.

"I don't trust you, ya know?" She said to the dog. "I like cats. They're not big and slobbery."

The hound wagged his tail and belly-crawled closer, so his chin was resting close to where her legs stretched out in the wet grass. He was staring at her with big, chocolate eyes, and she reached out and stroked the fur between his ears. When she was seven, a big dog bit her when she'd been trying to befriend it. She never forgot it. This dog, supposedly a puppy, was a rambunctious thing, but he had given her space. So, he was smart, at least.

She stood up to go in, and the dog jumped to his feet and spun out toward the water. He made a low-pitched sound, then looked up at her. She thought he was guarding her.

"Look, you. I don't need looking after by you or your boss, so you go on and get back up there."

She started back toward the cabin, and the dog raced ahead, leading her to the back door. She wished there was a deck out here, but beggars couldn't be choosy.

The dog was at the door. "Go on Hydro." She pushed past him and tried to shut the door, but he barreled past her. Her heart started racing. He was in with her. She didn't really know what could happen, but it was unnerving!

"Out." She pointed at the open door, and the pup ran over and hopped up on the end of the bed. "This is nuts," Jaime said. She shut the door and walked over to the bed where Hydro was curling into a tiny ball.

"I guess this is how you ignore someone if you're a dog." She pet the sleek blonde hair once more, and turned off the light. Being careful to keep her feet away from Hydro in case he woke up hungry, she was asleep in minutes.

Chapter 6

The following morning, the sound of a gentle knock on the door stirred her awake. Then the dog scrambled off her bed, barking, and Jaime nearly ran into the bathroom and locked herself in before she realized he was barking at the door, not her. She followed him slowly.

Hydro in her bed had been an odd experience, and her body ached from trying to fit in it with him. The mooch had been unmovable, laying on his back with all four paws in the air, snoring like a chainsaw, and her choices were to curl around him or sleep on the loveseat in the living area. She'd kept the bed, but barely. Thank goodness it was over, she thought as she rubbed her neck while pulling open the door.

Tad held a brown bag in one hand and a thermos in the other, and his hair was still damp from his shower.

"The boys are playing video games, so I thought I'd feed you since you kept my dog company last night. I hope you like bacon and egg sandwiches? They said they were hungry, so I made breakfast, but the boys have informed me they meant they were hungry for cereal. Are you game?"

Sleepily, she moved out of the doorway, content to drink in the sight of him. She could get addicted to looking at him, and that was a problem. "If there is coffee in that thermos, I might kiss you. Come on in." She looked down at her sleep shirt. "I'll just throw on some jeans."

He nodded, moving through the small space to the kitchen area. When she got back, he'd set out the plastic wrapped sandwiches on paper towels on the little café table and was opening a jar of homemade jelly stamped with the resort logo.

She nabbed the coffee he had poured her and inhaled. French roast. Good man.

"Good morning, handsome. If you plan to spoil me like this for letting that hound share my bed, I might have to get a bigger bed. He's a bed hog!"

Tad gave her a shocked look. "Hydro's not allowed on the furniture. He slept in your bed?"

His tone was almost wistful, and it had Jaime grinning as she shoved a corner of the scrambled egg sandwich in her mouth.

"This is actually quite good," she said. "What's on the agenda for the morning?"

"Well, I'm picking up a truckload of boys and we are going to practice at the city park this morning while it's cool. I figure I need to break them in easy since most of these boys are only playing since their parents make them."

"What about tomorrow? Can I help in the garden?"

"I don't expect you to help. I don't think your plan can work out. I've given it some thought. I haven't talked to the boys yet, but no sense putting you to work if I'm not sure I'll be able to hold up my end."

"Well, how about if I come check it out, just in case?"

He looked at her and shook his head. "Tenacious thing, aren't ya? All right, meet me there at eight in the morning. I'll be done feeding the cows by then, and hopefully I'll be able to roust the boys quick. If I'm late, you can just start watering." He gathered up the breakfast leavings and grinned at her. Hydro jumped up. "He slept in your bed, huh?" And he was gone, taking his hound with him.

Without the distraction she'd hoped for, she took Tad's advice and ordered everything she needed from Amazon and was having it shipped to her. Lana was right. Breaking away for a full day shopping trip didn't look to be in the cards.

She debated firing up her gaming laptop, but just gave it a wistful glance and got ready to go on down to the bar to see if she could find a place to spread out and work on the schedules for a few hours before she opened it up.

She could see the work crews swarming the campground, setting out trash barrels and swinging weed eaters, prepping for the weekend's crowds.

Her new tribe for the summer. Tribals might be a good nickname for the group of strapping young men, which she believed included about ten employees. Looked like half were on groundskeeping, and the other half were at the water's edge, flipping abandoned canoes over their broad shoulders and hauling them up the hill, muscles bulging.

A few groups of tourists were standing at the waterfall's edge, snapping photos, eating ice cream, and watching a handful of children doing cannonballs into the natural swimming pool above the waterfall's ledge.

She was determined to make this a wonderful summer. Attitude was everything, and so far, hers had been lacking. With a determination she was manufacturing, she settled in to take a chunk out of what was usually the least pleasant task she needed to do.

A few hours flew by as she made notes next to names that she wanted to follow up on, people who she wanted to talk to about new positions and wages. She left current schedules in place for the ones she didn't need to consult. With a few days under her belt, it was clear where the challenging areas were, and Lana's skeleton crew was going to need beefed up by two-thirds, almost. Should she have a job fair?

One thing she could see, this business would be a growing concern. Jaime felt it in her bones. Lana had really marketed and capitalized on the old Wilcox campground.

The challenges did not surprise Jaime. Recreation was a sexy moneymaker, and it helped the community, but innovative ideas faced opposition on the uptick around here. It was the main reason there were not a lot of young people in town.

The old timers were so strict... Well, they used to be, Jaime reflected, remembering seeing a few of them looking kind of chill in the last few days.

With a sigh, she started her last sheet, and penciled in a lot of hours next to her name on the bar schedule. Tucking the hard-won stack of schedules for the next two weeks in a neat pile for posting, she hoped revisions wouldn't be too bad.

She always implemented a rule that most owners kept after she left. All time is tradeable with supervisor approval. Unless you or a family member are sick, anytime you want a day off, just find someone to cover your shift and clear it with the boss, and you're golden. It reduced the hassle of organizing around graduations, weddings, and family vacations.

Mills Fall Resort needed more people.

She switched to her tablet and opened the emails Lana sent her with copies of the invoices she requested, as well as pertinent supplier info.

Jaime liked to look at everything so she could find all the best people to do the jobs in the best way. This was a more expansive project than she usually took on, and she'd need to be good, because the stakes were high for her friend.

This would take all her focus. She was going to have to work fast to stay on schedule. And this job needed done. If she lingered here... best for everyone if she did her thing and moved on.

When Lana began gathering support to expand their resort, she made verbal contracts with some locals who were talented producers. Old Mac with his greenhouse was her only supplier of fresh vegetables and he couldn't keep up with the demand they were facing, and it was still early in the summer.

Miz Harlow was the one responsible for the molasses and marmalade being used in the kitchen for recipes, and as she said, "We won't have any more 'til next spring, I reckon we should've thought of that before we sold half of it to the tourists."

The mushroom supplier was keeping up with demand, but his prices had risen steadily, sometimes every week. The butcher in town was also keeping up, but he was bellyaching about Falls Mill taking up all his time for a cut rate, and he was threatening to raise his prices, too.

When Lana stopped in to check on her, Jaime was feeling a little overwhelmed. A rare experience.

"Are you supposed to be up? How are you?" Jaime asked Lana, relieved to see her skin tone was back to normal.

"I'm good, girl." Lana nodded at the pile of schedules. "You look a little pale. How are you doing?"

"If you just say the word," Jaime replied, pulling at her braid, "I'll make a few calls and get a corporate supplier out here. The shortages are causing prices to soar, but a truck could be here in two days with the provisions you need."

It aggravated Jaime to be blocked by what she judged was locals trying to keep the upper hand, but Lana wanted to support her neighbors.

"We need the locals, Jaime, and we want them."

Lana wilted into the chair across from her, tired, and Jaime felt wretched. Her friend brought her here to take care of the details, yet Jaime was unable to enjoy the feeling of being in control, leaving her feeling restricted.

Lana went on, "From each step of the development of the dining functions, I've touted our locally grown and prepared cuisine. Do you have any idea how hard it is to get Uncle Jessie or Old Jake to agree to come out to dinner at a place that has the word cuisine attached?"

Jaime giggled, thinking of the two overall wearing lugs that were becoming a staple at Falls Mill. They sat around early, drinking coffee and exchanging gossip, then came back down to sit at the bar, snapping back a few beers, hitching up their overalls and checking out the crowds coming off the river. Then they'd amble out to their old pickups and presumably home to their beds.

"I can see that fine dining wouldn't be at the top of their wish list."

Lana grinned, "Yeah, for them it's right up there with putting on Sunday clothes and going to Branson for a shoe shopping bonanza. Yet, the wives keep making reservations, and here they come every weekend, dressed in their bibs with their ladies on their arms. They come because the butcher bragged on his chops, or they heard Emily has been baking pies this week. I want this community interested. When this mad summer rush dies down, they'll still be here."

"Okay, okay." Jaime scrolled the invoices again, thinking. "So, I have to figure out how to supplement what they give us, hurt no feelings, and get enough food to feed hordes of tourists." Jaime paused and looked at Lana. "So, how's your garden looking?"

Lana frowned. "Not a chance, sweetheart. I barely manage a few veggies for myself, and I'm eager to try making my own baby food. Garrett says—"

"Speak of the devil." Garrett stood in the doorway of the little office. He smiled at his wife, then looked at Jaime with a bit of chagrin.

"Uhm, I should have handled it, told them to vamoose, but then I thought I should come get you. Tad and Lug are having a shouting match in front of the store. It sounds like, well…" he shot Lana a mischievous look, "well, Lug has it in his head Tad needs to marry you, and settle you down. Tad seemed to think everyone should mind their own business."

Jaime dropped her head on her desk. She mumbled, "What are the chances they're armed?" She lifted her head and smiled a bit. "You know, put me out of my misery?"

Garrett and Lana laughed, and Jaime's smile felt a little more real.

"Okay, okay, I'll hose them down with a water hose. Lana, I'll brainstorm on this and let you know what I come up with." She slipped past Garrett, who seemed to eye the idea of cozying up to Lana. On the way through the door, without looking, she said, "And you two, get a room." She could hear them laughing as she headed to where the big boys were arguing about something absurd.

By the time she climbed the insanely challenging hill, she was grateful they were gone. She was opening the bar solo tonight. She'd like to do a little recon on the locals that had been drifting in.

It was a little awkward since she basically got run out of town on a rail. But the more she saw and remembered of folks, the less tense she felt. No one exactly greeted her with open arms. Lug and Tad were the only ones who seemed unfriendly, and Jaime supposed they had their reasons.

Tad searched the crowd, seeking long wavy hair, a high wattage smile, and a girl about her business. She was behind the bar. He was supposed to meet some of the other coaches here for a beer, but he came to see her.

He saw a few of the fellows seated at a table and gave them a wave before heading to where Jaime was the belle of the ball. The room was abuzz, and it annoyed Tad that all the stools around the hot bartender were taken.

Jaime was joking around with Bill Higgins, another coach, and Tad had to resist the urge to deck him. This place would turn into a hangout for horny drunk guys. He had already heard some dugout talk about her from the coaches, and they weren't sparing details.

The consensus seemed to be that Jaime was very friendly, and hinted several guys had a chance with her. There was a pool going to see who would score with her first. Tad was sick of it, especially since according to the polls, which he was not taking part in, he was a favorite to bang her first.

He had no claim to Jasmine Summers, and he wouldn't be making one. No way.

"Hi Bill," Tad said, muscling in on their conversation. Displeasure showed on the other man's features and an arrogant knowing played across hers. Blast the woman anyway. What was he going to say now? "Want to dance?"

"Bill here just asked for the pleasure, handsome, but as I told him, there are lovely ladies all around who aren't working who'd like to dance." She batted fake eyelashes flirtatiously and Tad thought it might be an alternate personality or something.

"So, doll, did you come in looking to pick up chicks? The redhead in the corner has had her eye on you since you walked in. I bet she'd like to dance." Jaime blew a little puff of escaped hair out of her face and gave him a cocky grin.

"Ah, such a witty bartender," Tad said. "I think I'll take a Corona, and how bout a round for my buddies over there," he added, pointing to the table.

"Oh, they're a lively bunch. You know, you can get a bad reputation hanging out with the rowdy kids?"

Didn't he know it? What was he even doing here?

"Don't worry about me doll, I have a reputation for ironing out the lines of right and wrong." He threw down beer money and a generous tip and said, "Have a great night."

Jaime seemed to enjoy his teasing, and he was reluctant to go hang out with the guys when she was being so friendly, but she was clearly working her butt off. While he talked with her, she'd mixed two drinks and sold about ten beers and an ice bucket of beer, which, for the record, she looked fantastic doing.

He'd let her work, and plan to help her. He knew he'd watch for her when she came home, maybe think of an excuse to visit before she went to her cabin. But he wouldn't come down and escort her home again.

As if he would chase the woman.

Hah, let Bill step on her feet. Tad was the best dance partner in these hills. He sat with the guys and he purposely put his back to her. No need to be caught staring. They talked casually of the prospects they saw in their kids on the field. When the topic changed to Jaime being back in town, he headed out the door, intent on getting out of there.

This was so frustrating. He wanted his sister to succeed. Lana was pouring her heart into making the resort a reality, but he wished she could have done it without bringing Jaime into their lives. He had seen nothing amiss with the woman, except for her casual attitudes about sex, but she didn't have that motherly vibe, so he needed her out of his head.

She stayed up all hours of the night. She cussed like a ranch hand. True, he cussed like the rancher he was, and both were good about watching their language around Cal and Ry. She vaped and probably smoked weed, too, though he hadn't seen proof of that, just heard rumors. Well, he smoked cigars, but that wasn't the point. Cal and Ry would look up to her.

And at the end of the summer, she was just going to disappear right out of their lives like the flighty thing she was. He needed more space, had to keep her out of their lives so they wouldn't get too attached. Just the boys, of course. He couldn't possibly become attached to such a…

She was so hot. He wanted to take hours pleasuring her as he explored her long body, the mole he'd seen on her back, the freckles on her chest… he wanted to indulge.

Too bad she was as toxic as she was attractive. Man, he wanted her, but he couldn't ask her to be somebody she wasn't. He wanted her, but the raw sensuality of the woman he kept looking at was making him nervous.

"Penny for your thoughts, cowboy." He refused to turn and look at her. She was wearing a skimpy little top designed to make men's blood boil. Her voice was enough of a lure… a siren from mythology. Only all her parts were very real, he felt certain.

"Baby, you can't afford my thoughts."

"Well, I saw you leaving, and I wondered if you'd decided?" Jaime had slipped up beside him where he was leaning on a railing outside. Hadn't he been leaving?

"We could do a two-week trial. That should get me over the hump," she said.

He wished he believed two weeks would do it. If two weeks would get her out of his system, he would agree in no time.

"Great minds think alike. The boys liked the idea, and I have someone to come up on the weekends and keep an eye on them while I work. I thought I would give you a month, Friday and Saturday night only. That will get you through 4th of July. After that, you're on your own. If I don't have a ranch hand in place by then, I won't have time to train them, so I won't have time for this. You give me two mornings a week to cut, rake, bale, and haul hay, whichever two days in a row that has no rain in the forecast, so you have to be flexible. And you water the garden 5 days a week. Take it or leave it."

Watering the garden? That was a stroke of genius. He wanted a garden bad, because his folks had always had one, but he may have messed up when he handed the boys seed packets. They planted all of them. He had no idea what was growing where, and by the sheer number of 2-inch-tall plants dotting the well-tilled space, it was all growing. Maybe she would know what the stuff was?

"I'll take it. I'm desperate."

"Quite a compliment, princess. Okay, see ya in the morning then. I'm due home."

"Princess? You can be a rude—so who did you get to stay with the boys?"

"The boys are with Lug. He came by to see how they got along while I was gone for an hour, so tonight is a kind of test run."

"My dad?" Finally, Tad looked at her, concerned by the panic in her voice. "You left your boys with him? Was he sober?"

"Geez, Jasmine, I think you might need to stop and look at Lug again. He's not the same man you left behind ten years ago."

"My dad," her voice held a sneer, but the catch in her throat belied it, "has no intention of letting me look again. He won't speak to me. Acts like he's never met me before. Whatever." She flashed her eyelashes up at him, not fooling him one bit. "So, I heard you guys were talking uphill earlier?"

She was clearly dying to be told what happened, but he wouldn't give her the satisfaction. Lug had just gotten the wrong idea and Tad lined him out. "We did. Later."

He left her at the railing. After all the weird stuff that had happened to him today, Tad felt strangely upbeat about his now more crowded schedule as he drove the short dirt road back to his ranch.

Chapter 7

Wanky country music blasted through the air, and Jaime forced open eyes crusted shut by the sandman. She stretched, pointing her toes at the big TV on the wall she had yet to turn on. Her computer received all her attention, as it had for the last 3 years since she discovered the greatest game on Earth.

She shocked her guild buddies last night when her Elven warrior resigned the lead of their hunting party. If she could get any screen time at all, she'd have to run solo.

She didn't remember when she got so consumed, but sometimes that was the way with her. An addictive personality, her shrink said. Sounded right, so she tried to limit herself to the things she got addicted to. It worked most of the time.

With a groan, she grabbed her cell from the pillow next to her to check the time. It was just after six in the morning. She'd only hit the sack three hours ago.

He started work so early. She was going to need to get some sleep, so pulling out of her group was the right thing. She'd miss it, though. Those elves, gnomes, and druids were like her family. But Lana was worth the sacrifice.

Tad was messing with her sleep, and that made her cranky.

She sat up, grabbed her robe, and wrapped it around herself. He could be a little more polite. She threw open her front door and watched him across the way for a minute. Tad was already in the garden, and the music seemed to be in surround sound coming from the house, blasting across the whole yard.

He was hoeing around the beans and she was pretty sure he was talking to them, too, or maybe singing to them. What a strange man.

Tad had a way of looking at her that reminded her of her dad's stern glares, as if his gaze alone could persuade her to do his bidding. When he was unguarded, she could hear the genuine acceptance in his voice when they talked. That put her off her game.

He was sexy as hell, and if he wasn't playing mind games with her on purpose, she was a unicorn. He knew he was affecting her, and it felt like she had no power. It was her habit to think mostly of herself, but she wanted his approval, which made her prickly.

She was used to calling the shots.

Tad seemed to be in the same boat.

Should be an interesting working relationship, since he nixed indulging in a sexual one. Shame…

She retreated inside and caught sight of herself in the little mirror atop the entry table. She looked sexy and mussed, her tiny robe hiding very little. Good thing the boys hadn't seen her.

She hated having to be so mindful. It was not her way.

What was?

She managed. Whatever it was, she could manage it. Tad Stone was not manageable. He did his thing regardless. She tested him, but he kept his cool, never rising to her bait and leaving her to draw her own conclusions.

Jaime smirked at herself and shook her head at the reflection. It looked cozy in his inner circle. Those he held dear seemed happy, and she wanted that. Maybe. She wondered what it would be like—family dinners and t-ball games and the kids scowling at each other over a toy… what would it be like to have that for herself? Jaime wondered and winced. No…

She'd looked for Tad last night, but he hadn't come to chaperone her home. Maybe he'd learned his lesson. Jaime couldn't remember feeling so confused in a long time. All that mattered now was that she lived in the present, not the past.

She shimmied into a pair of jeans, pulled on a t-shirt, pulled the t-shirt back off, added a sports bra, then her tee and some socks.

The lack of scene he caused last night in the bar had been almost embarrassing. Instead of forcing Tad to rise to the challenge by flirting, he'd left, and she'd had to listen to Bill Higgins' barely veiled invitations to join him in the sack, despite being a married man.

See, that should have ticked her off, that he would just leave. She was mad last night. Today, she was eager to go out and see what she could do to help.

This was all new, Jaime reflected as she pulled on her work boots. And it was growing on her a little, maybe. When she stepped onto the porch for the second time, the promise of working alongside him in the cool morning air was appealing, and she conceded with a sigh that she might enjoy herself. Maybe she could be useful. She was up now. If she could deal with the country music.

"I didn't think you were going to make it today." Tad didn't look at her, his attention focused on plucking blades of grass from between plants and casually dropping them in the bucket by his knees.

"Well, I did. I'm going to weed the tomatoes. You must be planning on making a lot of salsa." She didn't intend to talk about last night if Tad didn't bring it up.

"I've never tried. First garden, and I've never done any canning, but I figure it can't be too hard."

Jaime stared at him.

"This is your first garden, and you planted it full? Do you know how much work this is?"

He gave her a bland look. "Hence our arrangement. Might want to get busy."

Exasperated, she studied the jumbles of small plants that were everywhere.

"Did you mark the rows so you know what's where?"

"Uhm, I outsourced the labor to kids, so there's no telling."

Jaime felt her eyebrows climb up her forehead as she surveyed the scene.

"I got a bit of early lettuce and we've already eaten a salad or two off it. I'm not too great at gardening yet, but it seemed like part of ranching. My sister, now, she can grow anything. I'm not there, though, that's for sure."

He finally shared one of those warm grins that sent a little thrill right on down to her purple toenails.

"Well, I don't have a lot of experience either, but it looks to me like you're doing pretty good. I worked for this one restaurant where the owner had a little garden out back..." Jaime looked at Tad thoughtfully. "You know, if Lana put a small garden for fresh salads next to the restaurant, that could help offset these crazy rushes when they are running out of supplies."

"I don't think either of them has time with a baby on the way."

"I could..." With a conflicted heart, she amended, "I can't really, no. We'll have to find another solution." She'd been about to commit to growing a garden. Now, that was tied down, if ever anything was. She only had a small patch of the new grass tugged away from the roots of his tomatoes. She'd already done a lot of work and barely made a dent.

Like ranching, gardening was a labor of love and dedication, neither of which she was particularly ready to invest in.

He caught her mood and wisely changed the subject. "So do you have a date for the fireworks on the Fourth?"

"We'll be working, of course." She glanced at him nervously. Just when she'd given up thinking he was interested, he'd throw her a bone. He was a piece of work. She was halfway tempted to tell him Bill had asked her, but that was really shooting herself in the foot. Besides, she wanted to share a stupid basket of chicken with Tad.

If he kept resisting her efforts to get him out of her system with a roll in the sheets, her heart was going to find itself in trouble, and she didn't know what to do about that. Messy. It was Jaime's experience that deep relationships were like that.

Best to just avoid them. "Where are your kids?"

"The boys are off with your dad. He came early to take them fishing."

"Wow. My dad was here again?" Jaime asked, her feelings hurt.

"Yeah. The boys' Mom called this morning. She's going to pick them up for the weekend. When I called to tell your dad, he said he'd already promised them fishing today, so could he come by and pick them up? I should have everything squared away in time to help you out tonight."

"You're a dream come true, handsome. So, I can water every day this summer then. It's all good. It's best to do it before the sun gets hot, right?"

Why hadn't her dad knocked on her door? Well, she knew why, but he was being over the top. Once she got through the weekend, she was going to hunt him down so they could have words.

"Yeah, morning or evening, but not the heat of the day because they get all wilty looking. Experience talking." Tad stood up and stretched his arms over his head, and the corded muscles on his forearms flexed deliciously.

Pain in her…

"So, I've got to run some errands this morning, and I'll be out-of-pocket, but if you want to weed to your heart's content, then water before you go, I'll think you're the dream come true." He'd walked over to her, and leaned down to caress the leaves on the young plants. "So these are tomatoes?"

She laughed out loud. "You have no idea what's in this garden, do you?"

"Mmm, a pretty gardener and companion planting like you've never seen."

He rose and ruffled her hair, like a sibling, and smiled down at her. "All right, I'm out. See you down at the Mill at six tonight."

He headed to the makeshift garden gate and back inside while she stood up to browse the rather large garden space. Whipping her phone out of her pocket, she started taking pictures of the sprouts. Hard to tell much at this stage, but some, like tomatoes and peppers, had distinctive leaves, and they were everywhere.

She hunted down the water hose and turned it on a gentle spray that wouldn't knock the young shoots over. After about a half hour, she was still watering, and Tad came out looking edible and with a cheerful wave, climbed into that rusted out old pickup he drove everywhere and took off.

Another twenty minutes and she'd finally given everything a decent soaking. Crap. It had taken like an hour. What was she getting into?

She turned off the water and went out the gate, fastening it with pieces of the gate cut long to tie around itself, and debated between a nap and a walk to the river's edge. She decided on both and moseyed on down to the water first.

As she passed his outbuildings, she looked curiously at the mid-size shop sitting alongside the barn. She had a feeling she was going to spend plenty of time in that dreadfully huge looking hay barn. But a deal was a deal.

She was just stripping down to take a nap when a knock at her door surprised her. Jaime grabbed her grubby t-shirt and threw it back on with a pair of gym shorts, then peeked out the window. There was a gorgeous blonde at her door looking catwalk chic in a silk jumpsuit.

Didn't she realize she was in the woods?

Jaime pulled the door open curiously, expecting a cosmetic hard sell coming her way.

The woman's fake smile faltered when she gave her the once over. Jaime felt as naked as this gal was gorgeous.

"Ms. Summers, I'd heard you were back in Riverbend Falls and staying here. I'm with the welcome wagon."

Syrupy sweet snake oil just oozed from her. The blonde extended her hand and Jaime wondered if she was supposed to kiss it. Had royalty landed on her doorstep?

She politely shook hands. No need to be rude. Maybe this really was just a well-intentioned welcome wagon, despite her instincts. She glanced around for a dog, but to her relief, she wasn't about to get knocked over again.

"Cynthia Reynolds, you remember me from high school, surely? I was a few years ahead of you, but I remember you. All about you. Will you be staying here long?"

She glanced toward the house, and Jaime thought she remembered that Cynthia and Tad had been an item before he left for college. That was before her time.

But she remembered Cynthia. Maybe she'd had some work done. She looked different somehow. Maybe she was nicer.

"How kind of you to stop by. We'll have to catch up some other time, though." Jaime tried to keep the catty tone out of her voice

She gave Jaime's bedraggled state a snotty glance, and asked, "Have I interrupted you sleeping off a drunk?"

"No, Cynthia darling. You interrupted me sleeping on a sexy drunk. Consider me welcomed. Was there anything else? We're busy this morning… or is it afternoon? Hot sex makes me lose my grip on time."

Cynthia was so surprised her eyes bulged and her mouth opened, making Jaime think of a praying mantis in her chic mint Dior suit. Cynthia glared over Jaime's shoulder, no doubt wondering who would be foolish enough to hang with her. Jaime rudely stepped in front of her prying eyes and Miss Perfect backed herself up, gathering her dignity.

"Well, there's a lady's tea for the councilwomen on Sunday afternoon. You're invited and we're all expecting to see you there. It might be good for you to wear something a little nicer than what you're probably used to." She gave Jaime the classic 'you need help,' sneer. "So do come by my House of Design. I'm sure I can help you find something… tasteful."

She really did not like this female.

"Cynthia, darling, I'm afraid I don't drink tea, and I don't consider myself a lady, so no need to expect me at a lady's tea. You'll have to excuse me. I have a cowboy to ride." Jaime gently closed the door in her face.

With several hours to kill before her shift tonight, she opted for a grocery run. The cabin had a nice sized fridge in it, with a freezer, so she'd get sandwich stuff and some popsicles for the kids. All kids loved popsicles, and she should probably get the icy ones in case they shared with the hound.

No way she was going to sleep now.

She'd put all her energy into building a career, and knew when—if—she came back to Riverbend Falls, everyone in this town would see they were dead wrong about her.

She was not a hippy living off the system.

Lana wanted to set the record straight, but Jaime thought not. If they wanted to believe she'd run away to San Francisco for free drugs and sex, she could not care less. She'd enrolled in the Job Corps program and gotten her GED, advanced quickly through the basic and advanced culinary programs. She made more money on two jobs in New York last year than most of these farmers' houses cost.

Only… money can't buy you love.

Her bank book intimidated men, since she always insisted on covering her own tab, no matter how plush the indulgence. It was a control issue that kept things neat and fair. She lived out of hotels while on jobs and in-between. She never collected more stuff than what she could afford to leave and replace. It was a comfortable way to roll.

When the emotional tornado ripped through, it was best not to have any emotional ties to anyone else. A girl had to be ready to move at a moment's notice.

Her car was probably her most treasured possession, except her baseball cards, and she didn't know that prized collections fate. When she left home, she left her cards with the note, begging her folks to understand. She asked her dad to care for them.

She'd felt so sure of herself, then. She was going to be a famous chef, and she'd have a one-of-a-kind restaurant. Then she'd figured out money was what she really wanted and how to get it.

She called home after about a year. She was finishing school and knew she would make it. That night, she accepted she was the catalyst for all the disaster that had fallen over her friends and family. The three girls got arrested the New Year's Eve before, and Lana's folks were killed on the way home from the police station.

She hadn't known, and she ran away that night with a plan. So had Kat. She and Jake eloped and disappeared into the rodeo circuit. Jaime's mom was big on acceptance, and she was furious with Lug for being close-minded about the twins' wishes. When she realized both of her children were gone, she headed for a spa in Florida and hadn't been back.

Lug had told her in a dead calm voice that he had no idea where her mother or brother was, and not to call him again. She hadn't cared before, and he didn't know why she would care now.

He probably sold her cards out of spite and bought a bottle of good scotch.

The reunion with her dad had been horrible. He just didn't look well. His clothes were too big because he'd lost a lot of weight and there was so much sadness in his eyes. Why had her family splintered so hard? She knew her parents had been in love.

Stubbornness ran in their family down both lines, and Jaime and her twin, Jake, got a full helping each. Jaime needed to live in the present, not the past. She gave herself a little shake, cleaned up and headed into the devil's den.

Jaime was in Ralph's grocery store when she realized all the basic chatter inside the store had died. The silence distracted her musings about Tad. Having found a big box of icy pops, some lunchmeat, a small jar of miracle whip and a loaf of bread, she went for some lettuce and tomato and tried to peruse her surroundings. Perhaps it was a robbery, and she hadn't heard the stick 'em up command.

Her eyes lit on Ms. Goodwin, and she felt like she knew what was coming. The thought of being cramped up with all the biddies gave Jaime the heebie-jeebies.

Mrs. Rosati flanked her and the widow Donovan, and Jaime felt it very unlikely she was going to leave the store without an inquisition.

Mrs. Rosati laid the boom with a gracious smile. "Hello dear. We've granted you a temporary position on our event committee. You'll have to be sure to attend our meeting on Sunday."

Jaime dared not take the bait. "Good afternoon, ladies. I'm sure there's been a misunderstanding."

"Oh no," interrupted old lady Goodwin. "No mistake. We are in a bind with Lana being in the family way for someone to host the Old Soldiers Reunion planned for the end of the summer, and I nominated you."

"Well, I certainly can't accept. I'm needed at the Mill." Jaime was close to panicking. That was Lug's crowd, and he was a long way from happy with her. "I decline."

Mrs. Rosati smiled her matronly smile and went for the kill. "Everything is all worked out. Lana agreed to host the event at Falls Mill this year instead of the town park, and when she seconded the nomination to add you to the council, we created your position for you."

"No. I'm… I'm leaving at the end of the summer and that would…"

Ms. Goodwin was the toughest on her. She walked up to Jaime with her cane poking about and said, "Well, Lug's brat, all grown up."

Jaime pretended to be offended, but she loved the old woman scowling at her. Their relationship had always had a unique dynamic. "You must be mistaking me for my brother."

"Don't give me that, Jasmine Summers. I know it was you who kept knock-and-ditching my door and hiding my newspaper. I watched you, girl." She narrowed her eyes until Jaime knew she looked properly chastised.

"I did, and I apologize. My plans weren't always the most sensible. I'm sorry for any trouble I caused you, ma'am. If you'll excuse me…" Jaime was sorry, sort of, but she didn't plan to spend the day apologizing.

"Hold it right there, girl." Ms. Goodwin stuck her cane out, as if to trip Jaime if she moved. "I heard the Stone boy set his sights on you. What are you gonna do about that, girl?"

"It's Jaime, if you please, Ms. Goodwin." Jaime barely avoided rolling her eyes. No wonder she'd drawn the target of this old bird. "I'm planning to do my job and help establish Lana's business. Mr. Stone simply agreed to supply lodging while I was in town."

"Hmph. I personally missed your spunk around this town, and if the Stone boy has set his sights on you, you better think twice before moving on. That boy needs a girl like you, and his mama would've liked it. She always took a shine to your antics, telling stories at our meetin's."

Jaime's eyes misted unexpectedly. Kindness, she had not been expecting that. "Ma'am, I think—"

The old lady scowled, then hugged her.

"Seems to me you're doing a mite too much thinking and not enough action. I heard Cynthia asked you to our council meeting, and you sent her scurrying. I like that. You know she's had her eye on Tad since he came home, and she doesn't care much for you. Makes me like ya more. I'll meet you out front after church, and you can walk me over. You are welcome to come to church, but regardless, I'll have you sitting by me when the meeting starts."

She waved her cane at Jaime, and Jaime had the notion that she didn't need the cane to walk. It was a weapon. "I…"

"Good, see you then. Now, don't forget to bring some of those little cinnamon cakes you make. I love them."

She rounded up her cronies, and they left the store, like they'd been waiting to lynch her. Only…

This had been the biggest surprise of the day so far, and Jaime relished the look on Cynthia's face when she sat down by Ms. Goodwin. It would be worth talking about bingo and coupons for an hour. She hoped.

The rest of the gals had been pleasant and hospitable.

Ladies who had sons who needed marrying and parties that needed catering, and with Lana's baby news and Kat out of the picture, there was a shortage of willing women in the area. Jaime sighed. That was the beauty of cities. This little town was trying to get under her skin again.

Jaime stood there staring after them until Ralph gently cleared his throat, reminding her to check out. "The missus Goodwin is a tough old bird. I almost feel sorry for you, kid."

With a dazed smile, Jaime agreed, and was in her car and driving back to Tad's before she realized she forgot the lettuce. Darn. She'd have to poach from Tad's garden.

She decided she was in a bad mood. To be honest, little Miss Cyndi big tits was the first person to be openly hostile, so was she making headway. Did she want to?

Lana's plan to stick her in the middle might work well, give Jaime a chance to show off some of the polish she'd been earning over the years. And get the upper hand. The ladies would have no choice but to be charmed, and that might confuse the old gals enough to throw them off her scent.

Chapter 8

Tad laughed as the band launched into their last song, an ear-splitting rendition of an old Mick Jagger tune, and the crowd went berserk. He hadn't expected this to be so much fun.

He pushed a bar rag over a few water droplets that fell from the last beer bottle he'd passed over the counter. They'd given last call, but he'd sold a few more beers before he started turning people away, or selling them waters or sodas.

Had to have been over two hundred customers through tonight. It was a great crowd, and the band had kept them whipped up and dancing from the first set. Jaime was acting weird, though. She was all on, but her smile never quite seemed to reach her eyes. Hard to read.

The bar was small, and several times she'd backed into him, or stepped on his toe, and her luscious curves looked as good as they felt when she turned and walked straight into him.

With her height, their lips had been nearly touching, and he thought she was going to kiss him, with customers standing three deep across the tall wooden bar, but she'd just shot him some of that sunshine and danced around him, nimble as a cat. But the tension was like a weight in the air.

Finally, after the band had wrapped and had a round of drinks themselves while they loaded equipment, Jaime threw down her bar towel and gave Tad an appraising look. "You ain't too shabby, handsome." She grinned. "What do you say… let me give you a lift home?"

"I brought my truck." He stifled a yawn, and couldn't help noticing they had just become the only people left, and she was watching him intently.

"Good. Then you can give me a ride. I'm bushed."

She turned around and grabbed her backpack from behind the canoe. Tad waited, because he thought something was up.

"I've got early morning work. I'll be leaving before you get out of bed. How will you get your car?"

"I'll ride along, then you can drop me off here."

"Fine." He grudgingly grabbed his keys out of his pocket and handed them to her. "I'll get the lights."

Jaime grinned. "Every inch the gentleman, aren't ya?"

He stalled at the light switch. He was feeling it again. Vibes were flying off her like balls in a batting cage on speed pitch.

"C'mon slowpoke." She was still standing there in the door, in the dark, and she reached out and took his free arm in hers, nearly snuggling into him. "The moon is getting pretty close to full… think we'll have a bunch of crazies?"

"Yeah. It's been really hot." Even though the night had a cool breeze, his body temperature had spiked.

"The tourists are thick at the campground this weekend," Jaime said. "Lana says everything's booked and her waiting list is near full besides. I think she said they have over 200 canoes and about a hundred kayaks going out tomorrow. I hear you shouldn't swim after about ten thirty… half of what will come down the river will be spilled beer and pee."

She chuckled, a seductive raspy sound, and he could see the curve of her face in the moonlight. It was too much. "Look, Jaime, I…"

"Shhh…" Her breath was hot on his lips, and then he was tasting her. Her lips parted gently, but her tongue was more than ready for him. Tinged with the tangy flavor of the lager she'd just finished, her wild taste left him reeling. Her mouth was greedily stealing every bit of his reserve and her back pack dropped, freeing her other arm. When she pulled his body against her, he was lost.

She wasn't staying.

Reluctantly, he eased out of the gratifying grind and painfully abandoned the goddess's mouth. He was relieved he wasn't the only one gasping for air. She put his fire out quick enough, and her tone was enough to relieve the pressure in his groin.

"I knew you were holding out on me, cowboy. Why don't we knock down a few more beers and get naked?" She leaned into him completely, giving another tempting wiggle.

He stepped back again, against the wall this time, but took advantage of the space to reach down and grab her bag. Then he hightailed it up the stairs without a word.

On the way home, they didn't talk, but he couldn't tell whether she'd taken his silence as acceptance or rejection. Frankly, in the colored light of the new stereo he'd installed in the old truck last week, she was singing along with Stevie Nicks as if nothing had happened. Hmmph, women.

She was loud, but instead of obnoxious, she was vibrant. Aggressive and direct, not quite rude, and it was refreshing. She was blatantly sexual, and… it was driving him nuts.

Worse, she made it clear she wanted him. Briefly. That shouldn't bother him. She wasn't his type, but still it rankled. She'd be happy for a quick tumble, but be sure to stay out of her way. No strings. He wasn't any more special than any other chump she decided she might want to dally with. So why did Tad feel like a chump?

"Can we sit on your porch a bit before we turn in?" Jaime asked. "It's a great porch."

"Yeah," he said. "I'm pretty keyed up." They settled on the swing and he asked, "So, tell me… you love to cook, to bake, and you love pressure. Why bartending? The pressure, or the glory of being the most desirable person in the room?"

He chuckled, but it was truth, and she clearly knew it.

"Well, thanks for that, handsome, but you got your fair share of groupies in a hurry. I think it's whoever holds the keys to the beer cave." She laughed, and the hearty sound echoed across the yard. She seemed to think before going on.

"I do whatever needs done. Maybe think of it like this… you said you like the life of a rancher, and even though it could be profitable, it isn't always. Some days, the only real payment you get is catching a sunset at the end of a hard day, or seeing an eagle soar across the blue sky over a field you own. When these things happen, the money doesn't seem to matter as much as the feeling. Do you know what I mean?"

"I'm not sure." He leaned back, content to listen to her talk.

"When I get in the kitchen, the pleasure I get from creating meals from scratch is a real high. I've cross trained in several restaurants based on contracts and regulations, but pulling a pie out of a box deflates my spirits. It really doesn't matter where I'm working. If I can do it with pizazz and turn out a quality product, I'm being true to me."

She flashed him a wry grin. She was sharing more than she meant to, but he had a way of drawing her out of her shell.

"I can understand a little." He leaned back in the swing and gave a little push, swaying them gently. "But I wouldn't want to work in a slaughterhouse just because I like a good quality cut of beef."

She laughed. "Well, okay then. I didn't start out to work with liquor because I like it better than food, though I do," she winked at him and continued.

"I liked bartending because I'm a natural with people and then I started making a killing on tips behind the bar. Before long, I realized there was more I could do with the talent. Bartending's fun, but it gets stale. I found that by specializing in turning businesses around for inexperienced investors is not only highly profitable, it calls into play all the skills I'd been developing, so it was an easy call. The more jobs I did, the more I got offered."

"So, you came to Riverbend Falls for money, then?"

She looked chagrined and mumbled a denial. "No. I won't let Lana pay me."

He looked at her in surprise. "Not getting paid? But you're working like sixty hours a week! You're paying me when I help.

Surely, you're making some money."

Jaime shook her head, embarrassed. "Look, whatever. I'd do anything for Lana and she's afraid this won't work. I think it will. They've dumped a lot of money into this business, and she needs me to make it work for her. I'm sure she'd pay me, but I don't need the money. I just want to help. Besides, they still pay you."

"You surprise me again, Jasmine. You act shallow and uncaring, yet kindness and selflessness seep out of you seemingly by accident. Who are you, really?"

She unnerved him.

"I'm selfish and shallow, and I'm not even vaguely interested in changing my ways."

"I don't think so," he murmured, moving close enough that if she touched him, he'd be all over her. "I think you're beautiful, both inside and out. I think you don't want anyone to know because you're afraid it'll up the ante on how you're judged."

"Debating my personality traits is the last thing I want to do. Kissing is closer to the top."

"I think," his lips hovered near hers, then he drew away… "I think you're afraid to let anyone know what a special girl you are because then your act will be up. You'll be out of characters to play, and you aren't sure if you want to be left alone with yourself, Jasmine. I think you're afraid if you let yourself be you, you won't like you, and if anyone else doesn't like you, you won't be able to tell yourself you didn't want them too, anyway."

He leaned back against the truck again, delighted by the effect his analysis had on her.

She leaned against him, pressing her body so that it fit neatly against his in all the right places. "What I think," she said, leaning in as if to kiss him, wriggling against him, "is that you are a jerk." She pulled back. "I think you should keep your opinions to yourself, Mr. Sensitive. Go judge somebody else who wants to play along."

She was simply a distraction in a package.

He wanted her. Why couldn't anything be simple? Shouldn't he have met this girl first that inspired him in all the right ways?

But it had to be the way it was to have his boys, and he'd not trade them for anything.

Jaime looked away, but he'd seen the hurt in her eyes. Could anyone understand a woman as complex as the one in front of him? Yet, he was tuned to her. He marveled at the times in the past few days they had clearly been sharing wavelengths.

She was the best partner he'd worked with, sexual tension aside. If she would stop being her own worst enemy, maybe she could make peace with whatever was driving her away so hard, and there would be room for him and his boys in her life. Maybe he was being awfully wishful.

She pulled away, and he was planned to keep his hands off her beautiful shoulders.

"I know you've heard a lot of rumors about me, and I admit, they probably aren't rumors. But I'm not that girl anymore. I'm a little overwhelmed being here, because I feel responsible for a lot of chaos that spun out when I left. It hurt your family and mine. Look, I like you. Here's the but—no way. You're good looking, an amazing catch, but you're settled. It looks good on you. But it's not for me. We can be friends. We can be great friends, but whatever is drawing me to you, I need to shake it. We can't do an us. You have kids."

She waved toward his house, and hope evaporated. If his kids were a deal breaker, he was out. No deal.

"Right." He matched her soft tone, the wind from her storm subsiding. "G'night then." He gave one last glance out at what had been an epic nightscape, and headed inside, leaving her standing looking out over his yard.

Tad watched Jaime with suspicion the next morning as she'd shown up to water the garden, and she spent an hour out there weeding and tending what was quickly becoming a jungle. He needed to work on shoring up his makeshift fence a little, or he'd be feeding it all to the herds of deer wandering through every day.

Tad looked up as the siren emerged from his garden, and he ignored her as she moved closer to him, his dog following behind her like he was besotted. At least the dame was smart enough to stay outside the reach of the chainsaw. He finished the butt cut, kicked at the tree to roll it over, cut through the few inches on the top that freed the log, and killed the saw.

"Morning." Tad casually kicked at the freed log, still without looking up at her. He was a fool for getting lost every time he looked into her eyes.

"Can I help here? I'm about done in your forest today."

Tad looked her over, proud she wasn't wearing those delicate little slippers she seemed to favor. "I guess. There are some gloves on the tailgate there," he nodded, wondering if she'd put her long neat fingers in the oily old gloves, "you can throw this wood in the back of the truck. Leave the bigger logs. I'm trimming them for fenceposts."

With that, he turned his back to her and fired up the saw again, effectively killing any more conversation. The two worked together for several hours, and Jaime was clearly exhausted by the time he called it a day and offered her lunch. He'd worked the posthole diggers and she the shovel as they dug holes for the cedar fenceposts he'd cut, and they had seven out of twelve done.

No way would she be coming back to help finish this job. Her hands were red and puffy, despite the gloves. It wasn't an easy life he'd picked, and he doubted she'd want to play at it much longer.

"Bologna sandwich okay with you?" Tad asked as she followed him up to his house.

"I guess." Jaime seemed too tired to care, probably too tired to eat. "What time do you expect the boys back? I know you're being extra irritable today because the kids are gone."

"She's supposed to drop them off in the morning." He scowled and started attacking a loaf of bread. "If she hasn't misplaced them by now…"

"I can only imagine what it must feel like to share small humans with someone you don't like." Jaime moved in beside him and took the butter knife he'd been wielding to spread mayo. "Let me help with those. I'd rather have a sandwich than whatever it is you're doing to that bread."

He smiled at her, and his fatigue lessened as he let go of a little of his ticked off mood and leaned against the marble countertop. "Sorry. I don't mean to take out my frustrations on you. It's just…"

"No need to explain. I'm just here for the food." She ate a huge bite out of a piece of bologna, then tossed the rest of it at Hydro. The dog didn't seem to mind it landed on his head. "You work too hard for me to trade labor for room and board, so I'm grateful your sister got me in for free."

"I don't feed him people food," Tad said. He nodded his head. "But whatever. We all worked hard this morning. We've still got a few hours before our shift starts tonight, and I need something to keep my mind off…" he stopped himself and changed directions. "Want to go fishing, riding, maybe?"

"Uhm, neither. But I'd go fishing if it was instead of working on that garden fence. Why don't you hire someone, anyway?"

"Hah!" Tad laughed, a teasing gleam in his eye. "Have you had much luck finding dependable help for the restaurant yet?"

"No, but I have two more applicants on Monday afternoon."

"About that. Are you up for a little hay practice Monday morning? I have a small field in mind that we'll be able to bale up quick, and I can check out your technique. Finally, I'll get to give you some pointers."

"Oh you, dog. I'll do it, but only because I need your butt behind the bar tonight. I think I'm gonna nap for a bit. I'll meet you down there tonight at six, yeah?"

"Yeah." He watched her go. He liked her.

It was driving him crazy.

Tad was a hard man to live with, to love. He knew it. He'd met the boy's mother in a bar and spent the weekend together at his place. Then she'd split.

Eleven months later, Judith arrived on his doorstep holding what was undeniably his son and her luggage. The boy's strong Stone chin and gray camouflage eyes left no doubt to his paternity, and so Tad did what was right and married her. What a mess that made. Judith never knew what she wanted, but she knew it wasn't him. A law career, a family, a lover—she was insatiable.

When she'd wanted another baby, he tried to make a go of being a family, for Cal's sake. Children need siblings. Lord knew his sister was as hardheaded as a rock, but he loved her.

They'd married for the good of the child, and gave him a baby brother for the same reason. He'd do anything in his power for his sons. They were the best thing that came from his marriage.

Judith wanted money and power, and it was like asking Tad to be someone he wasn't. He wanted his kids to learn values and practical skills. Still, he'd been shocked when Judith and her lover and lawyer announced she was suing Tad for a divorce and custody.

She'd barely spent a day alone with the boys since they'd been born, deciding after Ryan was born that she wanted a career. In the years since, she'd used the kids as bargaining chips, and he'd financed the spendy ways of her and her lovers, and carved out precious time with his boys. That was no way to live a life.

He would go it alone before he could make his boys endure any more of the unhealthy patterns they'd been building, and he wouldn't leave them to her parenting.

Tad came home to Riverbend Falls to see if his sister would accept her inheritance, freeing it up for them both. He inherited a lot of land and sold enough to buy Judith comfortably out of pursuing custody. Shockingly, she'd even agreed to give him full custody if she could have the boys several weekends and holidays each year.

He hadn't expected her to actually come pick them up. Watching his kids leave as the boys sulked their way to her Mercedes had almost caused physical pain. He didn't trust her to have their best interests at heart.

He looked back at the large prefab house he'd bought to raise the kids in. The porch he'd built to honor his dad's memory. He had everything he wanted already.

He'd given up hopes of finding a mate that would match him for wit and spirit, and he was reasonably sure she wasn't out there. Now, not so much.

Here she was.

And his kids wanted him to make her his girlfriend, the flightiest thing to land in Riverbend Falls, a slip of a girl with eyes of a predator. Not what they needed.

Even the dog had sold out. He just rolled over when she came near and smiled that wicked dog grin he gave when he was thrilled. Traitor.

Chapter 9

Following the meeting on Sunday morning where Jaime had generously supplied the grand dames from around the neighborhood with her cinnamon puffs, she grilled her friends in the parking lot.

"What is it with you guys?" Jaime looked back and forth from Vivian to Lana. "That crew nearly hogtied me in the grocery store yesterday. What I just saw in there were a lot of accomplished women, and either of you would be perfectly capable of managing them and these plans. What's the real reason I'm being brought in on in this? And where is Kat? Not that I'm on a need to know…"

Lana gave Vivian a look, but Jaime saw it. Despite her mother mentioning Kat and Jake's troubles in her last letter, Jaime had stayed out of it. Meddling had burned her before, and she was a girl who learned from her mistakes.

Viv was pretty slick, and she guided the conversation just the way she wanted it to go. It was no wonder Lana turned to this vibrant woman for advice when she lost her mom. She made sixty-plus look sexy, and she was sharp.

Jaime did not trust her not to play more than one angle.

"Jasmine, darling, you have such a skeptical mind. Your brother and Kat haven't seen eye to eye in some time, but I'm sure you know all about that. The important thing is this event.

You know how history and heritage are to this town, and with Falls Mill to showcase us, we shall have an Event. It's the perfect time to honor all the soldiers who fought here on these grounds for freedom." Vivian waved her arm, and Jaime felt her heart flutter with admiration for the power of her charm. The woman was good.

"I still don't see why me." Jaime sighed. "How did I draw the short straw?"

Vivian patted her arm sweetly, moving around to her car. "We've missed you, Jasmine, and Lana here seems to think you don't plan to stay. A few of us, well, more mature gals, have decided you're just what we need for this town, so we'll be working on you to stay. Now you girls stay out of trouble, or not." She winked at Lana. "Call me if you need me." And she was gone.

Jaime turned to Lana and rolled her eyes. "Why are you encouraging them?"

"I want you to stay, too. Besides, Garrett is totally against me taking any new projects while I'm pregnant. I barely convinced him to let me come to work today," Lana said, and leaned over for a quick hug. "I know Viv didn't mention it. I don't want to surprise you, but Lug already offered to help with the coordination of the battle re-enactments, so you're going to need to work with him on timing."

"My dad? Seriously, we haven't even spoken civilly to each other yet."

"Well, you better get on it. Your mom will be here anytime. Shoot, I've got to run. I've got a quick checkup with Doc Robbins. Garrett's meeting me there, and he'll panic if I'm late. He is so excited about being a daddy. Better go let him and the doc listen for baby's heartbeat."

"Okay." Jaime gave her best friend a look that begged for understanding. "I don't like being railroaded. I can't stay, ya'know. But I'll do this thing if you feed me helpful hints for dealing with these women trying to arrange me."

"Okay, Jaime, I'll help you out, but I wish… never mind. Look, Doc fit me in special today because of our crazy schedule, but afterward, I could come over and we could just chill."

"Don't you guys want to work in the baby's room?"

"That was the plan, but I have a few things to do up at the store first, and I thought we'd have brunch at the Mill, but then…"

"No buts. You guys do your thing."

"Right. I'll probably see you later, then."

As Jaime watched her friend drive away, she wondered for the umpteenth time how things spun out of control when she hit Riverbend Falls.

Her mother was coming when? Jake and Kat were both out of pocket. Lug was mad at her for countless reasons and she was going to coordinate with him? Most distressing was that she was a tiny bit obsessed about her best friend's brother who had pain in his heart and children to raise.

Now Cynthia. Aggravating her would be a pleasure.

So, Jaime was a member of this little society all the sudden, huh? Had they forgotten who she was? The only question in Jaime's mind was whether she should remind them casually, or with a fiery bang?

Tad wasn't home when she got there. The disappointment surprised her, but she blamed it on the fact she was dying to share this crazy news with someone.

Jaime made herself a quick sandwich and sat on the back step of her cabin to eat it and watch the river. It was a little exciting. By being able to use Falls Mill's resources, the possibilities were endless for the reunion. Jaime was no fool. It was a public relations boon.

She remembered when she was a girl, little makeshift villages would sprout up around this annual party, since several skirmishes were fought right around here. It had long been a place for all the old soldiers to come and entertain their families with bold re-enactments. There was even a chuck wagon race— or at least there used to be. It never really mattered which side you'd been on. Everyone was just all mixed up and the improvised community had been full of love.

Her dad had always dragged his family to the events.

She knew the old soldiers still gathered, though many were aging out. The new age rolled in, and with it, a sense of goodbye to the rugged old days. But there were still some die-hards.

If she had her team in top operating order, the benefits of having these families at the resort for this event would create a ripple effect that might last for decades, creating new traditions for the same families looking for a unique form of fun.

A float, she thought. They'd have to have a float. For charity. Garrett and Lana might donate a portion of their rentals to the USO, and any soldier who wanted to float could do so for free. A guided float would get some people out on the water safely that probably hadn't been in a long time. Specials on lodging joined with dining packages...

So, this was just a temporary seat on a council to allow her a chance to manage this thing they would have asked Lana to do. And the event wouldn't mess with her plans to leave.

Sweetcheeks, hmph. Old gal was crazy if she thought some council seat was going to tether Jaime. She refused to be held to any plan that she hadn't crafted herself.

On a whim, she headed down to Falls Mill early.

She didn't see Lana's rig when she whipped her bug into her favorite parking spot under an old hickory, so she must still be at the doctor. Hopefully, all the news was good.

She walked down to the landing, the sun bright in the cloudless sky. Six days had gone by since Tad came splashing into her life, and the surprise of it still stuck with her as she looked at what would have been a wild and fearless jump over the spillway.

Stupid hero.

She strolled down, noting a few attractive young ladies flirting with the boat Tribe. Their sleeveless tees did a fine job of showing off the muscles they were earning, flipping those canoes overhead and lugging them up to be loaded on boat trailers.

Jaime waved absently at Cayson, one of the handiest folks Lana had on a steady payroll. She wished she could find someone half as steady for the bar. She wandered over to where the millrace harnessed the powerful push of the river's water power to study on the logistics of Tad's leap, and her problem.

She needed to harness the enthusiasm the resort was generating, and find them a bar manager. If she couldn't draw in workers, what was she even doing here? They were short on service, and that was worse than running out of food. A place like this had to be dependable for them to get the repeat business they would have to have to survive.

Garrett sure shot big when he laid out his plans. She poked around and found a flat stone and sent it skimming over the race into the river. Such a fabulous place…

"Excuse me, Miss Summers?"

Jaime looked up at one of the young ladies in bikinis who had been sitting on the rock wall when she'd walked up. She'd added a cover-up and a pair of pedal pushers over her suit, and tugged her wild red hair into a ponytail. "Yes?"

"Hi, I'm Kobi Larson. I know this isn't the proper way to go about asking for a job, but Cayson mentioned…" her voice quivered a bit, then looked at Jaime's friendly expression, and toughened up. "Well, I'm on summer break from college, and I'm looking for a job. I'm 21, and I don't have any official bartending experience, but my drink making skills are popular on campus. I have several recipes memorized and I'm a fast learner. Cayson said you were hiring bartenders."

Jaime lit up. Nicely done. She'd introduced herself, presented her skills, and showed initiative. She could be perfect. Jaime schooled her features. "How about we go over so you can have a look, and if everything seems like a good fit for you, we'll see about getting you on the schedule?"

"Oh, goodie," she squealed, bouncing a bit. "I've always wanted to try this. I was so sure this was going to be the most boring summer."

Jaime thought if the overwhelming cheerfulness didn't kill her, she might have just found her girl.

They'd closed the bar up tight on Sunday and Monday, and decided to keep the restaurant open Sunday afternoon for a brunch bar. They hoped to catch church folks and families heading home from their weekends.

She offered to work with Zack in the kitchen after her meeting this morning. She wanted a peek at how the restaurant was working, and the lovebirds needed a break. However, Zack ran her off after about 30 minutes, as he clearly had the small crowd under control. She'd agreed to come back and give him a hand with cleaning up at three.

Garrett's dine-in tickets meant success on Friday and Saturday night, thanks to Melanie's meticulous taking of orders and Lana's warm and welcoming hospitality. With Jaime and Tad below in the bar, her tribe had survived another weekend.

When she opened the bar Tuesday night, it would be with a lighter heart. Hopefully, she'd have some success with her interviews on Monday and be able to start a few trainees.

Kobi was a delight, and she had a lot of potential. She would have her work as a bar back next weekend to get a sense of the rhythm, then replace Tad.

She knew it was working him too hard, exhausting him to help her… Lana. But he was still doing his regular chores, and he had baseball season swinging in to high gear. She needed to cut him loose. She would see what she could do.

Her cell phone chirped, and Lana's message popped up, asking her to come up to the store. Maybe she was being released from her contract. That would be awesome. This place would go back to boring without having Tad annoy her at every turn.

No such luck, she discovered.

"I asked Lana to have you come on up, Jasmine. It's good to see you again."

"Mom." As much as she'd prepared herself, it was still a surprise to see her mother standing in front of her, swirling rainbows of silk and smiles. "Did you have a pleasant trip?"

"Really, daughter? You're going to make small talk with your mother?" Tabitha Summers used one of those rare frowns on her daughter and Jaime simply caved. Lana wisely used the opportunity to slink out of her office, leaving Jaime and her mom to their reunion.

"No Mom, I've missed you. More than… well, can I have a hug?"

Tabby swooped in, wrapping her daughter in a tight embrace. "It's about time."

Jaime didn't look to see if the catch in her mom's voice was tear infested, battling emotions herself. "Oh mama. It's been too long. I'm sorry. I'm sorry for…"

"Hush now, baby." She smiled, holding her daughter at arm's length, studying her. "You've grown into a beautiful young woman. I knew you would. It's so wonderful you've come home. I have missed this place so much. If your father wasn't as stubborn as his children, I'd have been home myself by now."

She grabbed Jaime's hand and pulled her into the office chairs, holding on as if afraid Jaime would disappear if she let go. "So, how are things going?"

"Well…" Jaime stuttered. Her mom was so full of life, a flower child holdover, really, and her zest for life tended to come out one part intimidation, one part inspiration. "I've been doing great. This job isn't going great yet, but I'll get it licked. I haven't had a restaurant environment to resist me yet. Last year, I did a stint in one of Emeril's restaurants that left me wealthier. I…"

"Oh fiddlesticks, Jasmine. Don't bore me with this nonsense. I read about your work, track your reviews. You know I'm a social influencer now. I don't give two figs about how much money you've made. How are you handling being back in Riverbend Falls? How's your father? Are you sleeping with Tad Stone? I heard you were living with him and he'd gotten a divorce. Have you been to the Stone's gravesides yet?"

"Oh, Mother. You never change. Wait, an influencer?" Jaime had tugged her hand back about the time Mom mentioned Tad and just shook her head.

"Direct as well. Let's see, in the ridiculous order you asked, let's see. Riverbend still sucks. I'm here for the money. Lug still hates me. He's adding to the grief this town is giving me. Tad Stone is a stubborn mule. I'm not living with him, I'm staying in his guest house, and he's not over his ex-wife yet, I don't think. And the Stone's graves, mother, really? They're dead. Do you think they care if I come stand on the dirt they're buried under? I don't think so. Feel better Mom? It's been ten years, and you poked me in all my sore spots. Happy?"

"Oh yes, dear."

Jaime tensed as her mom grabbed her hand again, the pressure of her grip heavy. The sting of her mother's words always stuck with her, her directness never softening.

"It's nice to see you being yourself. Even if you're lying. My baby may look elegant and untouchable on the surface, but inside is a delicate heart. I was terrified you had become as frosty hearted as your father. My girl, I've missed you. So, you noticed his position on the ex-wife? You are interested in him then?"

Jaime laughed, an explosion of emotion that gurgled into a kind of laughy-cryee teary thing. "Good grief. I've missed your craziness, Mom. So how have you been since you ditched Dad and ran away to Florida to, what was it, explore yourself?"

"That's my girl." Tabby nodded. "It sounds to me as if we've been equally miserable without our family close. I saw Jake just last month. He's… well, let's just say we put the dysfunction in dysfunctional. So, you haven't patched things up with your father yet? It seems I've arrived just in time. We'll see if he can manage being an arrogant turd once I start on him. He's not going to babysit my new grandkids by himself. I've missed him."

Tears filled her mama's eyes, but didn't spill. Jaime remembered her mom being able to do that on command, like an actress, but it still bothered her.

"He writes me the most tender letters each week, yet he won't come to Florida, and this place is etched into my soul. No more running for me. If he won't come to me, I'll bend. I've had enough. Besides, you are about to make us grandparents, right?"

"Mom, please. No. I'm still glad you're here. Where are you staying? I thought you had a cabin rented for the holiday?"

"Oh, I booked a room at the Inn and Out. So I have a base camp until I decide exactly what to do about your father."

Jaime grinned. "Good luck, Mom. I've got to go down and help clean up. Want me to scrounge you some lunch?"

Her mom hugged her tight.

"No, I'm on a mission. I just wanted to see you first." After another tight hug, she disappeared in a whirl of rainbow silk.

Jaime left the reunion with her mom, a strange sense of optimism tugging at her heartstrings despite her conflicting feelings. The loud and chaotic energy of her mom was strangely soothing, and she felt relieved to have another ally.

Did she want her family back together? Of course, unless she was required to take part in the drama. She intended to do her job and get out of here.

Would it be nice to not take a huge chunk of family resentment with her? Yeah. Like her mom, she was getting too old to play all these games, and she missed her dad. She felt sorry for him, knowing her mom's formidable energy was about to be directed at him.

Wild barking filled the air, and Tad watched as Jaime pulled into the yard in the cute ball of sunshine she drove. It was ironic that his prized navy blue 1969 Roadrunner had a racing stripe the same shade of yellow. He'd just tucked his baby back in the garage. He had parked the car for too long; and was glad he'd taken the time to open up the engine and hear its purr on the open road. He'd driven fast on the way to pick up his kids, hoping to blow off some steam.

He collected them from Judith in Branson. They'd actually had fun, and despite not planning to spend the morning driving, he was thrilled to have them home and happy.

They'd been asking about Jaime since they got in, despite being excited to ride in the Roadrunner. He'd let them both drive a little once they got to the dirt road. Cal first, then Ry, sitting on his lap. He knew he shouldn't, but the promise of it had redirected the conversation about her several times.

She got out and waved at them shyly. His team ran over and tackled her in fine fashion, and she even greeted Hydro timidly.

Tad joined them. "Hey, the boys have a surprise for you if

you can hang out just a minute?"

"Yeah, maybe." She glanced at the cabin, and back at him uncertainly. "Give me just a second and I'll come back out and check out the surprise."

Cal and Ry scrambled up from where they'd fallen in a heap with Hydro at the woman's feet, literally, and ran toward the porch where they left the souvenirs they brought her from Branson's popular theme park. Why hadn't he thought to take the kids there? Why had Judith thought of it? It wasn't her kind of place. She might be up to something sneaky. She'd bear watching.

The dog followed Jaime and then he came back a minute later, wagging his tail and carrying a piece of red popsicle. Tad rolled his eyes at her.

"What?" Jaime gave him her high wattage cool smile and handed him a grape one. She had cut the tops off two more blue popsicles, and she sucked on the other half of the red one. "I brought you one, too."

Man… she had point blank said she wasn't interested in anything more than sleeping with him.

He watched the boys give her the stuffed animals they'd picked out for her. Calvin's was a 6-foot purple snake and Ry gave her a stuffed dog the color of Hydro.

He was going to have to work on this. If he could let go of what he wanted in his heart, maybe he could treat her like a sister.

Then she could be an honorary Aunt Jaime to the kids and they could keep the memory pure of the small part she'd play in their lives this one summer. Because, whether or not he liked it, this off-limits woman was dug into his life like a tick.

Chapter 10

He invited her to dinner. She said maybe. Why? Why was he breaking his rules? What did he expect from her? She got up and peeked out the window just as the big Labrador burst from the back door of his house, followed by Cal carefully carrying a white bowl. Ryan put as much effort into carrying two bags of chips. Daddio himself had a cooler in one hand and a bag of charcoal in the other.

They made a delightful procession down to the picnic area at the riverbank, and as Jaime spied through the window, she saw both boys look at the cabin. Maybe wondering where she was.

Jaime sat down on the settee in front of the blank TV screen. She'd couldn't go. She was not blind to what was happening here. Those kids would raise their expectations of her, and then where would she be?

She had needed to take a deep breath to steady herself when they gave her the cuddly stuffed animals. She didn't want to break their hearts when she left.

Leaving. It was what she did. She never thought about it. Just built up and shored up wherever she was until she was no longer needed. It always happened. Then she moved to the next challenge. The stakes were too high here.

She wasn't going to dinner. She'd log in and see what was going in the virtual life she'd abandoned. Maybe hit the sack early. These early mornings and late nights were fraying her normally imperturbable patience, and she'd just catch up on a little sleep.

A loud knock at the door had her shooting up. He'd come for her. She had him. Yes! Thankfully, she was ready, in case. She was wearing a swimsuit under her cutoffs and tee. She'd spent too much time trying to look just this casual.

Jaime pulled the door open, expecting Tad, and found Ry and Hydro.

"Hi, Miss Jaime. Dad said not to bother you, but Hydro kept trying to come over, and I know he wants you to come out. I could walk you down if you don't want Dad to know you want to come."

"I…" Jaime laughed, delighted despite herself. "That would be nice, Ry. Aren't you the perfect gentleman? Just one minute." She went to the kitchen and picked up a package of chocolate chip cookies she'd found in her basket while checking out at the store. It remained a mystery when she'd added them to her haul. She kind of suspected old lady Goodwin of slipping them in on the sly. But whatever. She grabbed her shades and reappeared at the door. "Ready, Freddie."

"You're funny," Ry said, slipping his little hand inside her free hand. "Wait til you taste my tater salad. Dad helps me make it and we use a special ancient recipe. Do you like pickles?" He looked up at her uncertainly and continued, not waiting for an answer. "I don't like pickles, but Cal and Dad do, so Dad makes us bring them. Hydro's a weird dog. He likes pickles too, but he only likes McDonald's pickles, not the kind in a jar. But don't tell dad. Do you want to go swimming?"

"I might." Wow! Kid could really talk your ear off. "I might just grab a seat at the picnic table and watch for a while." Jaime gave his hand a big swing and let it go, and his smile brightened.

"Okay. I might swim now with Cal and guess what? You can be on our team if we play wiffle ball. You can help us beat dad."

Jaime ruffled his hair before he took off pell-mell to the riverbank, dog in tow, to join Cal and Tad.

Tad looked at her and Jaime knew for sure where his boys

got their heart stopping smiles. He told them to only play so far out and came back up to the picnic table, glancing over his shoulder as the bold Cal cannon-balled into the water, but quickly retreated to the water's edge while Ry did his move.

"I wasn't certain you were coming, but I'm glad. I see you brought dessert." He nudged the cookies. "A girl after my own heart. These are my favorite."

Jaime grinned. "Well, someone was looking out for you because they just appeared in my basket."

He looked confused, but picked up the charcoal and started spilling briquettes into the grill pit.

"What can I do to help?"

"Just do you. The boys already did the prep work."

He moved with an economy of motion, and Jaime tried to watch the boys, but she kept greedily sneaking peeks at Tad. She wanted him and she was unprepared for the lack of discipline her brain was engaging in. His kiss had set her on fire.

Lucky for Tad, it seemed to have the opposite effect on him. He seemed to have made peace with the idea of them being just friends. She wasn't so good with that, but sometimes you just had to let things play out for the best.

Dinner went off without a hitch and the boys ran down to look for sticks to throw for Hydro. She glanced shyly at Tad, as if he could hear her thoughts. She couldn't fall into the trap of routines. She fixed her attention on the conversation, hoping to find an opening to slip away.

"You've seen it…" Tad was saying. "It's like if you grow up here, you can't wait to get away. Your best employee is a maintenance man that was passing through and stayed, right?"

"You're my best employee, Tad," Jaime teased. "Seriously though, we got a boon today. Hired a super sweet girl to train for behind the bar. I was glad to see her because after a full week of hiring, I only have two new employees with a chance at two more tomorrow. I hope they are hirable, because I'm out of applicants. My best applicant this week for the kitchen was a girl who can cook Hamburger helper for twelve, and I hired her."

She shrugged. "My favorite applicant had more tattoos on

her body than hair. I hired her too, to serve drinks at the bar. I can understand why Lana was having such a tough time."

She picked up a leaf from the old oak they were sitting under and split it up the middle, then started parting out each of the little veins, creating a little pile of green confetti.

"Do you make so much money that you wouldn't consider staying on to help Lana?" Tad leaned back on the table with his legs kicked out in front and kept his gaze on the melee of action down at the water. The dog splashed around, trying to catch Cal while Ry just shrieked from behind him, and their laughter filled the air.

It was a question Jaime had asked herself. Maybe if she just took a year off flipping businesses and stayed on to help Lana build up her clientele and staff to match, but it really wasn't workable.

"I make a lot of money, and in the business I'm in, if your name isn't on the tip of tongues at restaurant conventions, you quickly get forgotten. My reputation is formidable, for now, but if I disappeared off the radar? I would lose my edge with the higher paying clientele and have to start in the middle tier and work my way back up."

"So, what do you do with all your money?"

"Well, I'm saving for retirement."

"Then what?"

Jaime looked at him. "I don't know. Settle down somewhere, maybe buy a house or something. I haven't given it a lot of thought." She pitched her confetti in the air, delighting in the simple pleasure. "I'm sure I'll figure it out."

"You've spent the last ten years fighting your way to the top of a career where no one will remember your name a year after you quit to amass a fortune you don't know what you're going to do with?" Tad crossed his feet and hooked his hands behind his head, looking up into the leafy overhang dappled with late afternoon shadows. Then he reached up and plucked a leaf and handed it to her. "Doesn't that plan seem off to you?"

Taking the leaf, Jaime said, "I'm really satisfied with my career. It sounds like a piece of cake, but it's remarkable. I'm on the move all the time, meeting new folks, always something fresh, so I'm never bored."

"Job satisfaction, huh? I think you like getting your hands dirty at the basic level. Isn't it your normal mode to fire existing problematic staff and replace them with more efficient employees?"

"Most of the time… well, yes. Firing people is just part of the job."

Tad smiled. "You haven't fired anyone here yet."

"That's because I don't have enough employees to fire!"

"I don't think so," Tad said. "Lana has been fussing about her few employees since she hired them, and I think everyone fully expected a pink slip from you. Instead, you've been teaching, molding, helping them to be better employees. I think you like it too. It gives you an opportunity to be more… I don't know, human."

She slugged him in the thigh, noticing how rock solid it was even at rest. The man had a delicious form. "I've never acted inhuman. Maybe I'm not the nicest—"

"I think you like being nice, Jaime." He sat up abruptly, bringing his gaze level with hers. "Maybe you punish yourself for being hard at work by not building yourself a sanctuary to de-stress. How long have you been technically homeless?"

"Give me a break. I usually sleep in plush hotels with room service and casinos if I'm lucky. That's hardly homeless. What about you, Mr. Rancher?" Jaime asked. This conversation had become increasingly awkward, and it was time to take control. She glared at him. "You were a suit, and you gave it all up to come hide in the hills and play with cows? Don't you like money?"

"Sure, it's nice, and you gotta have some, but no, I didn't think the tradeoff was worth it."

He looked at his children again. The dog was lying on shore watching them sift through pebbles and driftwood on the bank.

"This is the life for me. Sure, it's hard work, and there's not much of a payout, especially here in the beginning, but the work is honest and I feel good when I hit the sheets at night. When

we lived in the city, I never saw my children. I hated my job."
He shot her a quick glance and asked, "Are you sure you want
to hear all this?"

"Hey, I was just here for the food, but I'll take a story. I can
see it has a happy ending." She waved at the scene in front of
them.

Yeah.

"Well, my ex-wife and I fought horribly, and I was going
through life so pent up with frustration, I nearly made myself
ill. When she served me with divorce papers, it was like a chance
to start a life that held fulfillment. I was sorry to have failed her,
but it was killing me to fail myself."

"And you're always happy now?" Jaime asked, skepticism
lacing her tone.

"Always? Heck no. But most of the time." He reached up
and grabbed two more leaves, one to replace the second one
she'd shred, and one for himself that he just twirled by the stem
with his left hand as he talked.

"Do I feel good about my life, the work I'm doing? The job
I'm doing as a father? Yes. Undoubtedly. In fact, if I was poor
and didn't have my sons to provide for, I would be content to
wander off into the hills and live off the land."

He laughed. "In fact, when I was a boy playing here, I used
to dream that was exactly what I was going to do. A hermit's life
sounded so cool to me. My dad helped me build that cabin out
here in what was the woods then, and I would have been
perfectly content to go off grid and live here."

"The cabin is awesome, and actually perfect for one person.
I have everything I need. But it needs a porch." Jaime was
looking up at the cabin while she talked. He looked over his
shoulder at it, imagining him and his dad talking about the porch
it needed.

"It does."

"So, when did you get so serious?" Jaime twisted back
around when the dog barked. Cal had found a crawfish, and the
boys were chasing it out from under a rock at the waterline.

He smiled, proud of himself. "When Judith introduced me

to my son, that was the end of foolish daydreaming. Suddenly, I became responsible, and I tried my hardest to be what my family needed."

"All I've ever wanted was to make my family proud." Jaime sighed quietly. "It's odd, ya know? The night of the accident, my brother and I both abandoned ship, and it devastated my folks. Since my poor choices got us arrested that night, my dad blames me for the fallout, and I'm sure he's right. I just run my mouth sometimes and it drives people away. I've spent a good part of my life trying to atone for that one night—"

"I thought so." Tad reached over and laid his hand on her arm comfortingly. "Lana wrecked herself with guilt, and she said you and Kat were in tough shape, too."

"I've had counseling. I know it's not all my fault, but still…"

"I know. I blame myself I wasn't here," Tad said. "I was just another kid who couldn't wait to get away. If I'd stayed here in Riverbend Falls, everything would have been different, but you know, life is like that. We have to make mistakes to grow, even the painful ones."

He patted her on the knee and pulled his hand back. She wished he'd left it. Made her feel safer somehow. Which was risky.

"What do you say we go for a swim and then call it a night?"

Jaime tucked away the emotions he'd been stirring in her, desperate to hide from the pain. "Why don't you go on? I should get some sleep. The smell of the fresh-cut grass and the sound of the cows mooing in the distance reminds me we have hard work to do tomorrow."

"It's good for you." Tad grinned. "You needed toughening up. If you don't say yes to a swim, I'll sic Ry on you."

She returned his smile, feeling beaten. She hadn't been able to refuse the little angel anything yet. His big eyes were so persuasive. "You play dirty, Tad Stone."

"Yeah, well, I like to win big. Last one in's a rotten egg." He stood up, corded muscles rippling under his cutoffs and tank top with the motion, and strolled down to the bank.

She watched him as he tugged off the tank and dove into the

water. The boys barely waited for him to surface before they were hanging on him, trying to dunk him while the pup barked wildly on the bank, frolicking and splashing. The smile on his face proved to Jaime he hadn't lied. He was happy. She took a super quick dip, said her good nights, and retreated to the lovely little cabin built for a solo life.

Monday morning started out with hay hauling, and an idea about her dad knocking around in her brain. She hadn't said anything yet. She was still trying to decide how deep she should get involved with this. Jaime and Tad had formed an easy friendship, and except for the intense sexual awareness she kept indulging in, he seemed fine with the reality of her career. She would be moving on.

If Lug and Tad worked together, well, her dad would make a good ranch hand. Would she be meddling too much? They could help each other, Jaime could see it clear as day, but she needed to keep things as uncomplicated as possible. But like now, when the baler broke, her dad would have been on it.

The art of moving people where they were needed was natural for her, but it had sure backfired with family. She stretched in the sun to dip the tips of her toes into the water.

This had to be the most perfect place in the world. Owned by the perfect man, with the perfect kids… "Yeah, yeah, yeah…" she muttered to herself, pushing her shades up over the wild mess of hair her bun had unwound into. "It's a nice place," she said aloud, studying the bluff face up the river a bit.

Tad pulled in behind her and she had some delightful mixed emotions. She wondered what he would think if he knew her thoughts waffled between having hot naked sex in the grass or running into the air conditioning to hide from him. She thought she'd take the sex, but he had an armload of tools, which meant labor. Ugh.

"I was able to find what we needed. I should be able to have this belt back on in the baler, hopefully today." Tad grinned at her. "I see you took advantage of your break. Feel like making us some lunch while I thread this?"

"Sure." Jaime stood and picked up the lightweight long sleeve shirt she'd been sitting on. When Tad threw it at her and told her to wear it, she'd thought he was nuts, but it worked wonders to keep the hay chaff from eating up her arms. They were baling just over the ridge from the house in a field that faced a gorgeous bluff.

"I guess I'll walk up to the house. I've got peanut butter and jelly?"

"I have ham or roast beef and swiss, if that suits you? I'll take lettuce and tomato on mine. I picked the garden while you were sleeping in this morning, so you'll have to reward me by feeding me some of it. If you don't care, peek in on the boys? They are having a video game marathon this morning."

Apparently, he'd taken her silence for agreement because he was moving off toward the baler, whistling a song so off tune Jaime couldn't tell what it was. And why wouldn't he expect her to walk right into his kitchen and make a sandwich? It's not like he was asking her to have his baby. Just check on his babies. It was a simple sandwich and a simple task.

Well, not as simple as a PBJ, but she was certainly qualified. It's just... working in someone else's kitchen was intensely personal. Some girls had a no kissing rule that helped them not fall for someone. For Jaime, she stayed out of men's kitchens. But it was just a sandwich. And responsibility.

She paused at the back door before entering, prepping herself mentally. She'd walked through the kitchen a few times when she'd been invited up for Bar-b-ques, but she'd avoided looking around.

As she opened the fridge, Jaime was taken back to the summer she was fourteen, the smell of vegetables and leftovers filling the air, and the vegetable drawer looking like a work of art. Her folks had gone on a cruise and she'd stayed two weeks with Lana. She'd teased Mrs. Stone about organizing everything in the house, including the cat.

Lana's mom had such a neat sense of order, so different from her own mother's chaotic lightheartedness. Secretly, she was impressed, but couldn't see herself ever becoming a labeler.

Lana and Tad both seemed to have caught their mother's obsession with order and neatness.

She grabbed the sandwich supplies and slammed the fridge shut with aggravated force. See, this was too personal. Next thing, she'd be analyzing his cooking utensil drawer to see if they could share a kitchen.

She used the butter knife that she'd found in the dish drainer to spread stuff on sandwiches, acting ridiculously superstitious regarding the drawers. She made enough sandwiches for all of them.

She hadn't looked in on the boys yet, but she could hear them. They got crustless PBJ's, and she gratefully slapped the sandwiches on paper plates and grabbed a few paper towels. They cheered when they saw her, thanked her with full mouths, and had controllers back in hands in seconds. That wasn't so hard.

She went out to see how close the handyman was. Seeing he was on his way back, looking triumphant, she reached into the cooler he kept on the back porch and pulled them both out a frosty beer. She took a long pull off hers as she watched him walk up, wiping grease off his hands with a rag.

The brim of his hat bill shaded his eyes, but she could feel him wanting her. She was an excellent reader of pheromones.

"Looks good. Let me wash up." He disappeared and came back with two tall ice waters. "For dessert, so we stay hydrated. I think we can still get the lower field baled before you have to go do your interviews. You said two, right?"

She nodded, pressing the cool beer to her flush cheeks. Somehow, that had been more intense than riding a tractor.

"I'll have to work extra hard without my ranch hard tomorrow to get the upper field before the rain. It's a shame to complain about the rain because we sure need it." He took a big bite of his sandwich, looking out at the bright blue sky as if a thunderhead might pop any minute. "Good sandwich, chick."

"Thanks." Jaime was disappointed. Not a hint of that desire was scenting off him now, and he was talking about hay and the weather. Who would pick ranching as a career? Only a crazy workaholic, she thought, chomping into her own sandwich moodily.

A bit later, as they stacked the last square bale, Jaime collapsed on the hay, not caring that it was poking her neck. The cold shower she was longing for couldn't feel any better than just not moving. Blessed shade.

Tad stepped into the barn and sat down next to her and drained a bottle of water, handing her one. "You did real good, girl scout. Why don't you give up the restaurant scene and come work for me? The pays not the greatest, but it's good honest work, and it makes a body feel good."

"Ugh," Jaime replied. She hoped from his warm laugh he'd inferred that she meant he was crazy.

Chapter 11

After the first several weeks, Jaime recognized a pattern. When she arrived at Falls Mill in the early evening, her mom would show up shortly at the bar and grill for supper.

Her dad would drive up while her Mom was eating, but he never came down to join her. He made a beeline for what the boys called the story bench, and usually just whittled quietly or jabbered with the other old fellas who liked to do the same.

When her mom left, he would walk her to her car, then he'd leave, too. She hadn't seen them "together" yet, but something was clearly going on.

She planned to talk to her dad and Tad about the partnership they needed, and hoped her mom could soften Lug up a little.

Falls Mill Bar and Grill was hitting a good stride. While she was still on the lookout for trainable talent, she had enough bodies to work with now, and hadn't had to have the hiring fair, thankfully. She was busier than she'd ever been, and she was tired, but excited.

She still had Tad on the schedule, but Kobi was proving to be very talented, and Jaime had hopes of grooming her for the management position, despite her having one more school term to finish. So far, Kobi had happily soaked up the day shifts at the bar and grill so Jaime could work in the hay with Tad in the mornings. Then Jaime took evening shifts, and Tad helped her on the weekends.

She still needed to cut him loose, but she didn't want to. Despite the tender friendship they'd been building, there was a sexual tension that was getting in her head and taking over her dreams. But she had it under control, at least during the day. He was just good with the people, and they loved him.

The fourth of July was the following weekend, and they had a unique car show planned to draw in the daytime crowds. She could almost taste the courage that the weekend would require. All the rooms at the resort were full, and the venues for the bands were standing room only Friday and Saturday night. She had given her best effort, and now she just hoped it was enough to make a difference.

She walked to the door to watch her parents' odd ritual and stepped outside as her dad climbed in his truck. He leaned his head out his window and looked at her, but something was different. Rather than looking through her, he saw her.

He fired up his rig and drove over to where she was standing.

"Jaime," he said.

She nodded at him, shocked. "Dad."

"Story is you are in charge of the old soldier's reunion this year. Are you doing it, or are you pawning the work off on whoever you can find?"

"Finding people to pawn stuff off on is a trick around here, Dad."

He nodded and looked up the road. "Okay. Well. Looking good." He put the truck in gear.

"Wait. Dad," Jaime hesitated. "Thanks."

He nodded and drove away. Well. That was something.

Lug was… lonely. Like her.

She got another surprise the next morning. Tad cornered her as she finished watering the garden. "Can we talk?"

Jaime sighed. "Sure, what's on your mind?" She glanced up at him, but his expression was unreadable.

"Over dinner?"

"Tad, I don't think we should do the dating dance. It complicates our circumstances."

"Well, what do you say we change our situation…" He hesitated, then said, "I was only filling in until you found someone more capable behind the bar. After the holiday weekend, I'd like to step away."

Jaime's heart fell. Everyone in the resort liked Tad. She'd hoped a sense of family duty might motivate him to lend a hand in maintaining the formation, but it had been a stretch.

"Sure, no problem." Jaime gave him her best "Everything is okay," smile. She usually used it to let down people easy, so there was some irony here. "I appreciate you helping us through next weekend, but I can tell you, your fans are going to be disappointed."

Tad was nervous, like he hadn't even told her the bad news.

"What else is it? Do I need to move out of the cabin? I could get a room at the Inn and Out. My mom is staying there." Not as close as the cabin, but she knew she had an influence on his kids. Any father in his right brain would worry about examples she might set.

"Uhm, in a roundabout way. I'd rather talk over dinner." He pushed his hand through his wavy hair helplessly, and Jaime was morbidly curious.

"Just get it off your chest, cowboy."

"You're so pushy. Look, yes, I want you to move, but into the house, with us."

"What? Why?"

He fumbled in his pocket, pulling out a ring box. "Marry me," he said as he awkwardly tried to open the box.

"What?!" Jaime pushed the box away, refusing to even look at it. "Are you out of your mind? We barely like each other…" She looked at him suspiciously. "Have you been drinking?"

"Maybe I'm moving too fast. I might need a wife, and I have reasons I can explain over dinner…"

"I think you need to go into town and find yourself a nice girl. You're insane." Jaime turned off the water and folded her arms over her chest. "Moving too fast, ya think?"

"Well, I asked you to dinner."

"Oh, good heavens."

"So, come to dinner tomorrow tonight at the house with me and the kids?"

"No." She hesitated. "Maybe. But only because I'm nosy. Wondering what could be going on in your brain that you would propose so badly?" She grinned. "By the way, sweets, that's yes to dinner, and no to getting hitched, no matter what reason you come up with."

Tad was considering his lawyer's tip that his ex-wife was talking to her lawyer about Tad's living arrangement. His lawyer suggested Tad either get rid of the alluring bartender living in his yard, or marry her for respectability.

He was pulling the boys' new team uniforms out of the dryer when he heard someone pounding on the back door.

Freaking out, thinking one of his kids had been hurt while getting lunch with his sister, he sped to see what the deal was. Jaime was the trouble on his porch. It couldn't be noon and the woman looked half drunk.

"Is something wrong?" Perhaps she'd had words with her father. He pulled the door open to let her in and she nearly fell in on him. She caught herself and swore like she meant it.

"Let's have sex."

"Lady, do you kiss your mother with that mouth?"

She was looking at him like a wildcat aiming to eat him for lunch, and he was of two minds about it. He'd thought she was drunk, but decided she was just lubed enough for liquid courage. The rest of that wild in her eyes might be desperation.

"Look, you seem like a smart girl. You know I want sex, but I want more than that. Until you tell me how you really feel, this conversation's over."

He loved the fire in her eyes. The unquenchable lust she fired up in him. He knew she would be wicked fierce in bed and he wanted her. Would have her. But on his own terms!

"So, unless you want to sit down and have a rational discussion, perhaps…"

"You're the crazy loon who proposed. You think I'd marry you without knowing if you were good in bed first?"

It didn't take long for his brain to catch up with his other mind, but he'd keep the upper hand. He pulled her body against his, and his lips moved over her mouth, taking possession.

The kiss was more than passion as it hardened into desperation, their tongues and lips mating in a sexy dance that hinted of a sensual promise, finally breaking off into gentle kisses that made him want to keep her forever.

She was quite a woman. He held her tight, not allowing her to see how close he'd come to scooping her feet from under her and hauling her to his bedroom.

If he allowed her to make the rules, she'd reason it into an excuse why they didn't belong together. He had to keep her wanting.

"Look honey, I'm just trying to get along, and when you come in here demanding something from me, whether or not I want to give it to you, you're not going to get it. I'm not one of your pushover pretty boys, like you seem to want, but I like you, sure enough. My boys like you."

He frowned at her then, knowing they all liked her too much.

"We have our opening game today in a few hours. Would you like to sober up and come watch us play ball?"

"Sober up?" She scoffed, then looked abashed and tugged out of his embrace. Backing out the door, she paused and asked, "I might have to work, but just in case, what time does it start?"

Tad smiled. Chalk one up for the home team.

Jaime pulled into the parking lot at Riverbend Falls' ball field and wondered why she was doing this to herself. And the sweet family she had innocently crashed into this summer.

Tad's truck was parked over by the home team dugout, and Jaime could see Hydro's enormous head hanging over the side of the truck as the dog watched the game with interest.

She wished she felt half as relaxed as he looked. She sighed and left the haven of her car. Coming to this game was a turning point. She was now officially inserting herself into this family dynamic, even if she had no idea what her position was to be. It's not like she could be a big sister to the boys while she was actively trying to get in Tad's pants.

Or shorts, she thought, as she spied him standing just behind first base wearing the team uniform. He looked edible. She spotted Ryan waving at her from the dugout as she ambled over to pet Hydro behind the ears.

Being little, Ry wouldn't get a lot of time on the field, but he still loved being on the team. He'd confessed to her he was a little scared the ball would hit him in the forehead like it had in practice, but he swore her to silence, not wanting Cal to hear he was afraid of anything.

She waved back and then found Cal standing on second base with his helmet a little big on his head. He was staring at the batter and kept glancing at his dad, looking for a sign to advance base. At seven, he was pretty fast, and having been coached by their dad, both boys were extremely good at sliding into bases. Jaime had been watching them practice in the backyard, and had even joined them in a few good-natured games of wiffle ball.

She leaned on his truck casually and watched. The air was so humid, she couldn't believe the boys could run and play this time of day, but they seemed not to notice.

When Tad came back into the dugout, she watched him give the boys a pep talk. They had struck out at bat, and Cal had only managed to steal around to third base before the ump called the third out.

"So how come you all aren't sweating like crazy?" Jaime asked Tad as he moved off to the side of the dugout close to the truck to let his boys take the field.

Tad smiled. "It's our secret weapon. We practice in the heat and I let them drink all the Gatorade they want. If there's minimal whining, we do ice cream after practice."

"Pretty sneaky, Mr. Stone." Jaime pulled her gaze from his rugged frame and looked over the field as the boys ran into their positions. Ry looked tiny out in left field and Cal was practicing grounders with the shortstop. "What's the score, Coach?"

"Since you're here, I'd say it's a score for the Stones. The boys both noticed you pulled in. Me too." His gaze on her felt heavy, like he was trying to read her mind.

"Well, how could I miss the first game of the season? A baseball nut like myself can't ignore an opening day invitation." She shrugged, maybe a little defensively.

He released her from his stare, and looked at the boys, then hollered out a few changes, "Sam, move up, Cal, move back," and a few things like that, waiting for them to comply before he turned back to Jaime. "I thought you might have to work?"

"I took the time off, okay, geez. Yes, I wanted to see you, to see them play. I'm here, all right? I'm going to watch from the tailgate over here, Coach, so you can keep your mind on the game, and if there's minimal whining, maybe I'll pay for the ice cream today."

She grinned impishly at his expression, then joined Hydro in the sultry sun to enjoy watching her... the boy's play.

Tad was glad he parked behind the dugout, because he was really getting a kick out of watching her. If she was trying not to distract him, she shouldn't have worn those cutoff shorts. Her tan legs tempted his imagination, and the way they climbed all the way up to create a perfect rear end would have him drooling if not for the fact he was supposed to be a role model here.

If she'd sat in the bleachers with the old men, he'd have had to go get her. Her t-shirt was attention getting in team colors, she'd obviously given thought to coming, but it was the breasts she was sporting on that lush frame he noticed. She was smoking hot.

She was going to have ice cream with them. If he could keep his mind off her long enough to help the boys win this game, he wouldn't have to give them as much of a pep talk afterward.

Maybe he could even get her alone for a little while to tempt her some more after the boys hit the sack tonight. They were playing hard, and they'd probably sleep well. You had to love baseball.

It was a close game, but Riverbend Falls pulled it out 1-0. Cal was jubilant, and his excitement was mirrored by the entire team. The boys were all swooping around, their parents moving in to congratulate the boys and the coaches.

The parents were ecstatic after winning their season opener, and one parent offered to buy the team pizza at Mickey's. Tad groaned inwardly. He should be thrilled since he'd had his doubts, but the alluring woman who'd been absentmindedly stroking his Labrador's chin distracted him. He'd have to get a rain check from her. No way would she want to go to a pizza parlor with ten kids and a random assortment of parents.

"Did you see me get a run, Jaime? Didja, didja?" Cal ran over to Jaime with Ry right behind, and when she crouched down, Tad barely checked the urge to see if he could see down her shirt. What was he, fourteen? Geez, he thought, scrubbing a hand across his face, and re-tweaking his ball hat.

"I did, sport. I had my fingers crossed, but I didn't need to. You were fast." She reached out and gave him a high five. "And you, Ry! That was an amazing throw in the fifth inning. Fielder extraordinaire. Bet you boys worked up quite an appetite. Sounded like someone even thought you were worth pizza."

"We are. You're coming too, right Jaime?" Ry looked at her with those trusting eyes, and Tad was caught between worrying they were all getting too attached, and hoping Ry could sucker her.

"Course I am sport, being in the cheering sections hard work, too." She shaded her eyes and looked at Tad. "Shall I just meet you all there?"

"You can ride with us, Miss Jaime. Me and Ry want to ride in back with Hydro. He likes to come everywhere so dad lets us ride back there sometimes, and a couple of the guys are gonna ride with us, right Dad? You can sit with Dad in the old person section, because he's gonna drive real slow."

Without waiting for an answer, giggling like hyenas, they ran back to the dugout to collect equipment. Jaime smiled at him and said, "Good game, Coach. I wasn't sure if you wanted my help a few times, y'know, remembering you were on the field in a major important game."

Tad shoulder checked the hottie, then glanced at the boys. "It'll take me a few minutes to get everyone organized… if you don't mind riding in the old people section." He winked at her and glanced down at her legs appreciatively, "I can bring you back for your car afterward."

Jaime looked at her little yellow bug and back at the truck. "You'll be coming right past the ranch. How about I drive my car there, then I'll wait by the road and you can pick me up? I'll probably feel too fat and old after eating pizza to want to drive. Sound good?"

Her eyes twinkled, and Tad wondered why he couldn't have met this girl… Never mind, he scolded himself.

"Yeah, that sounds good. We should be about twenty minutes."

She slapped him a high five, and he watched her walk to her car, then turned back to corral the hooligans. One of the other two coaches, Bill Higgins, who was Gavin's dad, caught the exchange and intercepted Tad.

"Good game, Coach," he chortled, "and I ain't talking about baseball." He nodded up the road to where Jaime's car was disappearing. "So, I reckon you got to be the first in town to tap that honeypot… is it as good as she makes it look?"

Tad scowled. "Back off, Bill."

"Heya, coach, no reason to get all huffy. So, you think you can put Gav on first base next week? His momma wants him to try first base, y'know, like his daddy played."

Gavin did not have very good hand to eye coordination, but he had a great arm, and Tad felt he excelled on third base. "We'll ask Gavin if he wants to practice on first some, then go from there."

"Can you drop Gav by the house when you're done feeding him? Me and ma are looking for a little alone time ourselves, ya know what I mean?" Bill wiggled his bushy eyebrows suggestively, and Tad stifled a groan.

Gavin's parents were not Tad's favorite. Bill coached with an eye for his own interests, rather than the kids, and Gavin's mom had hollered criticism at Gavin from her lawn chair behind the batter's box for most of the game.

Tad didn't care for it. But it was Little League, so if he wanted to punch Bill out, it wouldn't be in front of a bunch of impressionable young boys.

"Sure Bill, Gavin can ride with us... I'll drop him off in about an hour."

Chapter 12

Jaime somehow ended up hanging out with the boys alone on Sunday afternoon while Tad made an emergency grocery run. They had survived a wild bar scene last night, but they had handled it. She hadn't decided whether to stay for dinner.

Ryan and Calvin were hosing each other with water guns in the backyard, and Jaime sat on the back patio in the warm sunshine, watching them play.

They liked to pretend their sleek portable was a cell phone, and Ry had insisted on bringing it out in case his dad called, but Jaime had commandeered it to keep it dry. When it rang, she answered it.

"Stone residence."

"Hello, this is Judith. Theodore, please."

Theodore, huh? "He's not here right now. May I take a message?"

"What do you mean, he's not there? I can hear my children running amok and screaming in the background. Let me guess, Theodore couldn't wait to get custody, and now he's dumping them on a babysitter. I knew he was being hypocritical." She harrumphed, and Jaime just raised her eyebrows, knowing this must be the ex, not knowing what to say. Then Judith said icily, "Yes, I have a message for my husband, but I'll deliver it to my son, not some teenage gum chewer."

Now Jaime was getting irked. "Ma'am, I declare... them

boys is amok, and they's all wet. They been playing in the water and the dirt, and I'm not right sure they're muddy lil hands ought to come over and talk on the tellyphone. Ma'am."

The woman hesitated, and Jaime imagined Judith thinking about muddy little boy prints in her house. "Fine. When do you expect Theodore back?"

"Ma'am," Jaime was really getting into her southern accent. It was more fun than a barrel of money. "I reckon the mister'll probably come back today. He was to bring us a hog to butcher so's my family could eat supper. Y'know, I babysit for hog jowls, and…"

Judith interrupted. "Fine, fine. Tell him to call Judith." She sounded her name out carefully so Jaime could understand. Jaime almost giggled, but covered it. "Yes'm, I'll tell him…" she told a dial tone. The boys ran closer and targeted Jaime, now with super alien ray guns, and they soaked her pretty good by the time she reached the water hose.

Tad watched her running from the boys as they hosed her with their super soakers, and she occasionally turned and blasted them back with the water hose. The sight was amazing. She hollered and laughed as the boys chased her around. Her melodramatic dives to the ground caused eruptions of laughter as she leaped back up and chased after them, arms outstretched like a beast, wagging the hose with her. For a girl who didn't have kids, and professed not to like them, she was a natural.

When the boys spied him, they dropped their guns and raced over, Hydro in tow. Taking in the vision of a super soaked Jaime, he wondered if this was what it could be like. He'd missed seeing his sons happy, and had to admit he'd missed loving a good woman. Stepping out, he gave his boys high fives and pet his hound on the head.

"Fellas, I see you're playing, so I assume you finished your chores?" He asked, knowing the answer. He'd rather play with Jaime than do his chores, too.

"No, Dad," they said in unison. Cal explained Jaime wanted to see their water guns, and then they had to fill them up to show her how far they squirted.

Jaime ambled over and hopped up on his tailgate, while and Tad sent the boys in ahead to change into dry clothes and start straightening their rooms. Even though he understood, rules were rules, and with boys, you had to be firm. Girls too, maybe…

"So, did they behave for you?"

"Just like boys."

She looked fantastic wet, and Tad got a little carried away thinking about it. Her next words were a cold shower, though.

"Your wife said to tell you she called."

He scowled. "Ex-wife. Damn." He walked back to his truck and grabbed a cigarette from the door panel. "Did she say what she wanted?"

Jaime was clearly having fun with this. In a high, clipped voice, she said, "For Theodore, her hypocritical husband, to call Judith." She copied Judith's tone precisely when she'd enunciated her name.

"I'm guessing from your perfect imitation that you answered the phone? Did she ask you if we were involved?"

"Uhm, no sir, but don't you worry, none. She knowed I was just a hayseed baby sitter. That was when she decided you were a hypocrite." Jaime looked down at her wet clothes pointedly. "Anyway, I delivered the message. I might have also told her you paid me in hogs."

He looked at her with a cross between awe and glee. Judith might have just ticked off someone savvier than her, and Tad was glad to have a sexy hellcat in his corner. Maybe. He wanted to kiss her, but stopped himself. He wanted so much more.

The resignation in his voice implied it would be disastrous for his ex-wife to think he was involved with her. That stung.

"When I see that look in your eyes, Tad, you make me want." Jaime rubbed her forehead, feeling frustrated. "You know this can't go anywhere, this thing, with us. Those children need a mother. My lifestyle—"

"Could change if you wanted it to. You don't have to do

anything but be yourself." He poked her in the arm. "Try to lighten up. And watch your cursing unless you want them both to swear like army brats."

"Lug's worse than me," Jaime protested, wanting very much to lighten up. It seemed like everything required big decisions. Couldn't anything just flow for her, like usual?

She had been wondering if it was mental self-sabotage. She knew from experience she had a problem with success. It was why she'd loved the freedom her job granted her. She never had to accept management, and she was always in charge. She used what she almost considered magic to come into a business and create structure and flow where there was none.

Maybe being around Tad was what had her on edge. She kept seeing herself in their family, and she knew better. It could hurt many hearts. She was not a settling down girl, and she couldn't comprehend choosing a guy with a package deal.

Except, she was thinking about it too often for comfort. She needed to put some physical space between her and them.

She hopped off the tailgate. "I'm going to head out."

"Don't run away from this, Jaime." He stood as if to catch her, but he didn't reach out. "I'm not asking you to be their mom. They have a mom already. This is dinner at my house with me and my sons. I understand the hesitancy. We're worried about getting attached to you, too. You've made no secret of your intentions and we'll respect them. I've talked with the kids several times about this, and with Judith—"

"See, they will compare me to their mom, won't they? They are children, and they're going to associate my leaving with abandonment, and I can't do that to them."

"I want to be with you." The emotion on his face belied his simple words. It had been hard for him to say, and he knew she would shoot him down.

"I can't commit to this, Tad. I'm all in for a quick romp, but the children change everything, and my parents are acting crazy. Maybe I should move out of the cabin. The proximity is… challenging."

She was going to have to be hard. He was looking at her like a whipped puppy, and she was going to make it worse. "We have to stop this. Kissing is out. I like it too much. I don't think we need to be taking our meals together. It's too… familial. I care for you guys. That's why I think this is important."

"How do you think Cal and Ry are going to handle you rejecting them early because you don't want to get hurt? I don't see how it will be harder for them when you leave than it would be if suddenly you just quit hanging out with us. We're just living, babe. The pressure on you, you're putting it there."

"You play dirty. I didn't think of it that way, and I don't appreciate you pointing it out. It's rather inconvenient."

"Caring about people can be a little inconvenient," Tad said dryly. "Now, c'mon, it's dinner and a conversation where I explain what an idiot I am. You should enjoy the show. No big deal. Say yes."

Jaime sighed. "You're a pain." He was so compelling, she wanted to say yes to him all the time. She'd have to keep working on a way to get out of this snare. Everything in this neck of the woods was complicated.

"I think I'll go get cleaned up then. I'm going to take you up on that dinner invitation."

The man annoyed her. And why was she always soaking wet whenever she wanted to use her assets? She shouldn't have answered the freaking phone. Should have just put Cal on. Why did she pretend she was the *babysitter*? Riverbend Falls always made her feel like she couldn't find her footing.

A rock star, that's what she was. She had a sweet career. Six figures a year, easy. Now, a babysitter. And the job she was here to do? She was going to have to get serious about upping her training schedules. Right now, they just needed to get through this weekend. Then everything would calm down and she'd have time to train.

So she could get out before she got stuck.

She might not have left ten years ago, but it was the only way to stay out of that backwoods jail. Everyone around here had always pinned her with the blame for anything that went sideways, and that New Year's Eve was no different. Folks around here were just looking for a way to put her in her place. When Jake and Kat eloped the same weekend, that only left Jaime and Lana. And no one would blame Lana.

Jaime stood up, determined not to start a pity party. She needed solutions. That was her gift. If she could work things out for Lana, the confusion would dissipate like a fog, drifting away with her when she left. Jaime would be sure to take care of herself. What would make life in this town any different after just one summer?

She stared at her reflection in the mirror, her eyes tracing her own image. She felt guilty because she had fallen for this family. Her operating mode was shot, and she didn't really know how to handle the parts of the conversations that might come next.

Another part of her was strangely happy. She wasn't the type to get married or be a mom, but somehow those boys had pulled her into some strange realm where kids could actually be likable. Go figure.

Not that she was considering marrying their demented father. Was she? But she wanted his story. She wanted more than that. But she couldn't give all they needed, and it sucked.

Her pantsuit was boring and lacked any flair. She saved it for the occasional funeral or luncheon. With her hair pinned into a chignon, she looked businesslike. Perfect. She rubbed her face, devoid of any makeup, and blew out a deep breath. Insane.

What had gone wrong? Ever since he yelled at her in the river, they'd been drawing closer and closer despite her attempts to manipulate the relationship's path.

She leaned in to study her complexion. A straight up invitation for sex had never failed. And that kiss. She'd never kissed quite like that, either.

She'd lost herself in it, forgot about being in control and allowed herself to languish in the sheer pleasure. Was Tad such a game changer? Was he playing a game at all, or was it like he said, everything up front?

She turned from the mirror and sat on the bed, pulling her ankles up lotus style. Why was she letting him under her skin?

Jaime didn't think anyone had ever proposed to her that wasn't drunk or on the other side of a bar.

Why had he?

Could he really think there was more to her than she thought there was? She knew better.

She had a brief window of time to finish the job, and she could feel the pressure on her shoulders. Spending her spare time with Tad, where she could hear the birds singing and the wind rustling in the trees, made time feel like it was slowing down. One minute, then the next minute, and then the hours were gone. If only they weren't adding up to some of the most stimulating hours of her wild life.

She had to put an end to the ridiculous craving she'd been having for a life she could never fully embrace.

After delicious takeout pasta from Rosati's, with cheese raviolis for the boys, no sauce for Ryan, Tad frowned at Jaime seated next to him on the porch swing. The boys and Hydro were watching a movie, and the house was quiet.

She had to admit she was enjoying aggravating him. He was clearly way out of his league here. Finally, she had something he wanted, and he didn't like it.

He'd been high handed for weeks now, setting down rules, expecting her to obey because she was on his turf, and now it was her turn.

She smiled innocently, batting her eyelashes, and ignoring the teeny voice inside her that warned this might not be a game she wanted to play. That this game's stakes were higher than any she'd ever played for.

"I told you if we face facts, this could be simple." Tad shrugged and tugged at one of her wayward curls. "It's obvious you like me, or you wouldn't hang out here when every cowboy in town would like to take you out. You know I want you, but I can't risk being viewed as a poor role model, so I can't just sleep with you. I don't really have time to date you, but we like you… The boys want you, and I enjoy having you around, so if we just hook up, it fixes my problems, on paper."

"I don't know if I should punch you now or later. You're

telling me you want to marry me, not because you're overcome with passion, but because it would look good, be convenient. Not because you think I might be the one, and you don't want me to get away, but because you really wouldn't have a lot of time for me. We should just do it. Tad, darling, who taught you how to finesse a woman?"

"I'm not trying to finesse you, Jasmine!"

Tad growled, but he absently curled a ringlet of her hair around his finger, totally finessing her.

"If I was trying to finesse you, I would have thrown you down in the hay barn and given you the only thing you really want. I'm trying to negotiate with you."

He gazed at her, a flame of emotion in his eyes, while his words extinguished her heat. How dare he consider her so… shallow?

She had been pursuing him, and she knew when she made eyes at a man the way she'd been making eyes at Tad, there was no mistaking her intent. But he could have had the courtesy not to be so dumb about it.

"No. That's my answer."

"Do you want dessert?" He asked, a cool expression sliding in to shield his soul from her.

"Dessert? What are you, nuts? You can't just change the subject like that!"

"I can. I bought the good cannoli from Mrs. Rosati."

Finally, Jaime said, "I'm not a romantic girl, Tad, but I—"

"It's fine, sweetheart."

His expression made her blood boil. Although she was unsure of the emotion behind it, she knew it couldn't be good. He looked so tempting, despite how reserved he'd become.

"Your answer was an apathetic "no," so I think we can just forget about this. Too bad you don't want to try the cannoli. They are out of this world."

Jaime was miffed, but what else could she say? Then she had an idea.

"Let's look at this from a different point of view. You want Judith to see that this life you have chosen for them is good for them. That's your end game, right? If you keep the unfeeling attorneys out of this? I have an idea, and I want you to hear me out." Jaime glanced at Tad, and he was still staring out at the yard, pushing against the ground rhythmically to make the swing creak just so. It was now or never.

"Hmm…?"

She liked when he was lost in thought. He puckered his lips, making the little cupids bow on his top lip wiggle under the rugged mustache he wore to hide it. Tad was devastatingly handsome. He'd done a number on her, for sure. She couldn't believe what she was about to propose.

"Okay, so I've been watching things go down this summer with Judith and I think…" She threw her hands up in defense when his attention snapped back to her and he scowled, his pupils glinting in the light gently shining from the living room. "Just wait…" Jaime begged him and continued when he nodded slightly.

"What if… Hey, do you want to check on the kiddos, and then maybe walk to the water? I think better when I can skip a rock."

Tad looked at her and shook his head. "Yeah, I get that. Give me a minute."

He returned with a blanket under his arm. "Okay, they're both crashed and the movie still has an hour left. Hydro will keep an eye open. Let's go."

Tad relaxed as she started walking, and though he returned his gaze to the darkened yard, she knew he was listening.

"I think Judith wants you to have the boys. She as much as admitted they're too much for her to handle. She likes control. I recognize it because it's a trait I have."

Tad groaned, but threw the blanket on the picnic tables top and sat on it, overlooking the moonlit water. She joined him, and the gentle sound of the river moving on calmed her.

"See, she hates the idea you chose this lifestyle of ranching to spite her, and she's probably afraid of losing any regard her sons have for her because they are fitting in to your lifestyle, where they weren't in hers. That adds rejection to loss of control, and it can be uncomfortable. Just by doing you, you're proving you're right, and showing the boys your way is more rewarding. Boom, you're pointing out to the boys that her lifestyle, wealthy and career minded is wrong. She can't stand for all that."

His warm voice was calm, which was a good sign. "What are you, some kind of gossip columnist? You sure have been paying attention to the nuances of my failed marriage."

"I can't find someone who gets me, since the one who can't stand me doesn't want me to be happy." He let out a cynical chuckle. "Judith gets offended easily. I put my heart and soul into trying to make it work for that woman. I was stuck wearing a suit and tie to work for six years so I could make enough money to keep her in shoes and handbags, and she rarely said a pleasant thing to me or the kids. We'd just ruined her life, and she couldn't forgive... but you figured all this out, right?"

He looked at her, then reached out and took her hand. "Where are you leading with this?"

In the light breeze, Jaime's heart was hammering, and the sensation of warmth that spread from his hand to her heart when he took hers was almost too fast to bear, but she had to keep going, not try to jump him.

"Invite Judith here for the weekend, treat her like royalty, and show her how great the boys are doing. I'll throw together a fancy event at the restaurant, like a wine tasting, and she'll get to mix with some of the better off folks in the Falls, and we'll reassure her you're doing her a solid by raising the boys here."

"How do we convince her I'm doing her a favor?"

"You'll ask her input on the woman you're gonna marry, so she can be confident the woman won't be competing for her son's love."

Jaime got it all out there, though she was no longer sure whether her heart was pounding because of what she was saying, or his touch, but it was about to hammer out from under her tee shirt. Could he hear it?

He was silent for so long, then he said something that she didn't expect. "Might work... who's the woman you would pick for me to marry as a mother for my sons?"

"I thought… well, me?" He'd already proposed, for heavens sakes.

"You turned me down, and you have a very convincing list of reasons, Jasmine, why you can't and won't marry me." He arched one of his thick eyebrows at her. "Did you devise an angle where the arrangement could benefit you?"

"Don't be a jerk, Tad. I'd do anything for those boys." Jaime was getting mad. She'd thought it would tick him off she was interfering, but she hadn't imagined he would backtrack on the idea of marrying her.

"It's a package deal, Jas. I can't let you marry me because you feel sorry for us, or you think a fancy party can fix things."

He looked her over, hard.

"Even dressed as plainly as you can, your fire lights up mountainsides. I don't think you can convince Judith you're not competition. And what happens at the end of the summer when playtime ends for you?"

"I don't feel sorry for you." Even she could hear the hurt in her voice. "Sometimes my ideas aren't the best."

"I married once, out of duty. I wouldn't wish that on your tender soul. You're a beautiful woman, and I wish you loved me, but I've watched you. The passion's there, babe, but not the staying power. You'd start feeling trapped and… I can't do that again. Not to me or the boys."

He let her hand go, reached up and pushed a stray hair behind her ear tenderly.

"Thanks for the kind offer. It shows that I was right that you hide a big heart in that long, strong bod. I'll think about the wine tasting. It's an idea. I'll think it over and see if I have anything else I can use to convince Judith. Thanks for thinking about it."

He smiled kindly at her, but the smile felt different, vague.

And that was that. Jaime felt everything was wrong, but it was too late. Though they sat companionably listening to the rush of birds flittering in the trees, she felt him closing her off, out. Worse, he was right.

She got caught up, just for a minute, with being needed.

She wasn't into getting married or being a mom. She would keep reminding herself of that. She was enjoying herself so much with the boys… she was sure they could get Judith to agree with Tad's decisions. What was Jaime's move when the acting was finished? She had no idea.

She gave his leg a gentle pat and tried to bring some levity to the situation. "All right, well, whatever I can do to help. So, you want to fool around?"

He chuckled. "I don't think so. Seems like now would be a good time to turn in." He stood, and she reluctantly got up too, but he started walking away. "Good night."

"Well, good night," she said, the words heavy in the darkness. Jaime watched Tad leave sadly, her gaze following him until the porch light went dark and the only sound she heard despite the night noises was the echo of his door shutting with finality.

Chapter 13

Jaime's gaze drifted moodily out the kitchen window Sunday morning at the water churning over the waterfall below the restaurant. The gray morning was a harbinger of things that could go wrong today.

She, Tad, Kobi, and Staci had survived the two nights, but by late last night, when they gave last call, it was literally because they were out of supplies. Jaime had made sure they were fully stocked, and every bit of it had sold.

It was after ten on what she'd dubbed punishment day. They had scheduled a few large parties for that afternoon, then they would close shop and everyone would go watch fireworks at the baseball field. Success had been so close.

Zack, the cook working the upstairs lunch shift, called in arrested, and Ally, her waitress for dining, called in late. Garrett was driving out boatloads of floaters, so the kitchen was unmanned.

It seemed the Sheriff still knew how to spot trouble. Zack was in his mid-twenties and had a temper problem. If he stayed on his meds, he was fine, but if he started skipping them, he seemed to end up in a fight somewhere. It was hard to be mad at him because he was usually defending some girl from a pushy boyfriend. Last night, he got the girl, but today Jaime needed him behind the grill, and he was cooling his heels for six more hours.

"Jaime?"

Kobi called her name from the quiet dining room. They weren't open yet, but the party of fifteen red hat ladies were coming at eleven, when they opened, and they wanted to start with coffee and a meeting before having soup and sandwiches.

"In the kitchen," she called out.

"I heard Zack called in. Can I help here?"

Kobi was turning into a godsend. After a few weeks at the bar, she'd expressed a desire to pick up more hours in the kitchen working prep, and she'd filled in for Zack twice already. She was competent.

"You will not believe this, but I can't find milk or bacon. There just isn't any. Ally is coming to wait tables today, but she called and she's going to be late." Jaime took a deep breath. "Can you watch for our gals and get them seated and served coffee? I already have place settings, waters, and some carafes on the table. About to brew some decaf, just in case."

"I'm on it," Kobi said with a giggle. "A few of the ladies already pulled in and are browsing around the resort. Wait until you see these hats. Outrageous!"

Jaime smiled, grateful for energetic help. "I'm gonna look one more time." A quick survey showed more than bacon missing. Lunch was going to be rough. She stepped out of the walk in and consulted this week's delivery. She could tell there was an issue right away; she had made a list of what she had collected and what she needed to cover the downstairs, but the backup order she had hung up was missing. "Ah, geez."

"Pretty bad, huh?" Kobi leaned back against the counter, the coffee made. "What can I do?"

"Let's see if we can get through the next few hours." She opened the homemade soups she'd put together for downstairs and divided them for both parties. After that, they'd just have to be sold out. "Can you call up to the country store and find out if Lana has any bacon for sale for campers?"

"You bet."

Alone in the kitchen, she wondered if she could survive this job. The success of Mills Fall Resort was a source of pride for Lana, and Jaime had much to thank her for or else she might have just walked away. The stark contrast between the number of jobs available and the amount of people looking to fill them was obvious.

Garrett stepped in, two packages of bacon in hand, accompanied by the swoosh of the staff entrance opening. "So, Zack pulled a doozy?" he asked.

Jaime sighed. "I reckon. Kobi's helping out, but I have bigger problems than just being short-staffed. Oh, thank you for the bacon." Jaime whisked the soup thickeners, trying to catch the right consistency. "You're a lifesaver, but you're lucky we're almost done. Our grocery supply has run out. I have a plan, but I can't leave these Kobi alone to handle everything. I could kill that kid."

"I have to take full responsibility," Garrett said. "I told him I'd call the order in, and I forgot." He fished her folded up order out of his back pocket guiltily. "I'm having fun in here, but I'm going to have to admit, I'm not balancing it very well. What can I do to redeem myself?"

His honest embarrassment tugged at her heartstrings.

"I'll tell you what. Let's call Tad and ask to raid his garden. I need a gallon bag of potatoes, tomatoes, lettuce, cucumbers, and snap peas as fast as I can get them. I started a short list over there. Look around for anything else that might fry up fast to put on special. That will help distract from the fact we're out of the menu items. We'll figure the rest out tomorrow."

He nodded. "I doubt we say it enough, Jaime, but we really appreciate what you're doing here. It is working. I just really didn't listen to my girl when I planned so big. I know you told her we should just close today, but I really wanted the extra exposure for the car club, and Zack wanted the hours."

"Go on," Jaime said. "And thank you for the kind words. Don't worry, if we survive lunch, you've got this!"

Then she called Tad to convince him this was a worthy cause for the abundance of his garden.

Hours later, the rush ended. It was done, except cleanup. She'd found a few puny steaks and fixed them for Garrett and Lana, who were also finally at a breakpoint. Literally.

It was possibly the only decent meal either of them had time to eat this past weekend. Garrett was done driving buses, and the Tribals were just loading boats off as they came in. Lana left Mel and Jane to handle anything that might come up at the office.

They had survived the big weekend. Jaime didn't get nervous, but she'd been worried. At noon, the Ford T-Bucket Hot Rods had come through. The local car club paraded their unique model T's through about twenty towns and they stopped for their lunch break in Riverbend Falls.

Jaime had catered the self-serve lunch of soup, sandwiches, chips, and drinks to the group of 50 downstairs on the open-air deck. Luckily, she ordered enough supplies for her downstairs project, so she spread some of it around upstairs as well.

They really needed one person to oversee all the orders.

The car club president, a retired politician, promised to talk up the resort to all his friends. His endorsements were a big deal, but Jaime didn't worry. Even with limited resources, the event was a success.

But, man, if she wasn't understaffed again. She felt like every time she tucked away the stack of applications she'd garnered in the beginning, someone didn't show up for work. The excuses ranged from "ran off," to "got married," to now, "I was arrested, so I couldn't call and let you know I'm not coming." Frankly, Jaime was tired of hiring. She certainly hadn't had to worry too much about firing people.

She pulled her apron on tight and got busy cleaning up. She'd done more work on the floor in this gig than she had in probably five years. It came as a bit of a surprise that she was enjoying it.

Lana rushed into the kitchen with a stern expression, her hair flying behind her.

She'd only sent the steaks out a minute ago, so there must be something wrong. This summer was shaping up to be a real dog, and now she couldn't even cook a decent pair of steaks.

"Jasmine Summers, you've been holding out on me. What are you doing with your life? If you can create food this savory, why are you wasting away behind the bar serving drinks? Please, say you'll reconsider and cook for me always. Say it now, so I can enjoy that plate of heaven before it cools. Tell me you'll stay, or I won't enjoy a bite of it, knowing I can't keep you."

Jaime shook her head, amused. "Go eat, little mama, and quit worrying so much. I'm sure that everything will work out in the end."

Jaime was hoping it would happen soon. She was thinking about admitting defeat. She might not make this happen. Her dad's disappointment was weighing down on her, and she couldn't stop thinking about the Boy Scout next door—she was about to break.

How do you keep a seasonal business going with enough employees to make it through the summer and not leave them struggling in the winter? She was determined to solve the puzzle. She couldn't leave Lana without the trustworthy staff she needed with a baby on the way. If Jaime couldn't do her job, it would be better if she hadn't come and brought false hope with her.

"Shoo, shoo. Don't make me regret putting on this apron."

Lana was already headed back toward the door, but she didn't let the matter rest. "Think on it. Come sit with us. Take a break."

"Another day, Lana. I'm flat busted. I'm headed out as soon as I can."

"Fine." Her voice floated back through the swinging kitchen service doors. "But I'm not giving up."

Jaime had wiped down the last tables and was confident everything was back in its place. She finished locking up just in time to feel the rumble of the bridge as the antique cars did their victory lap, their vibrant colors and unique styles of Model T's creating a beautiful sight before they drove away. A gorgeous navy blue and golden yellow hotrod idled into the parking area, and she had the thought that the classic looked stellar parked next to her golden yellow bug.

Tad stepped out, and from the pheromones he was putting off from this distance, he was hot for that car. It must be what he had hidden in the little garage that he rarely used. He walked over to her, wearing a huge grin.

"Hey sexy, want to take a ride later?"

She almost blushed. "Oh, you know I do, handsome. What year is it?"

He began to tell her, but then Calvin rushed into her line of sight and she saw her dad was having a difficult time trying to keep up with Cal and bring Ry along as the small throng that had been sending off the riders dispersed.

Calvin thundered to a halt before them as the last of the T-Buckets fell into line to leave, "Dad, those were awesome. Can we get one? Can we? I like the red one and the green one and the yellow motorcycle can be my back-up. Did you see the blue one, Jaime? It had lightning bolts!"

Calvin was crackling with enthusiasm, but Ry seemed a bit down. His gloom dampened his features, and he wasn't imitating his brother like he often did when he was happy.

Jaime shoved her bag over her shoulder and looked to her dad, who was holding the young man's hand, and Lug's head bobbed ever so slightly as he gave a slight shrug. Jaime crouched down in front of Ryan and touched her fingers to his forehead like her mom used to do, but he felt normal. She gave him an encouraging smile. "Didn't you like the T-buckets, sport?"

"I guess," he said in a small voice.

Jaime tried again. "Did you bring your swim trunks so you could go swimming before the fireworks tonight?"

"Yeah, but I don't wanna swim." He looked past her at his dad, then ran to him and leaped into his arms.

Jaime looked at Calvin, confused as she stood up. "What's wrong with Ry?"

"Mom called this morning. She's coming to pick us up again next week, but Ry doesn't want to go. He's afraid you'll leave while we're gone."

Oh, man, this was out of her league quick. She had to be careful. "It's only the middle of summer and I said I'd stick with

Lana until Labor Day, so I'm not going anywhere soon."

"That's what I told him," Calvin said. "I even showed him how to count the days on the calendar, but…"

Tad shook his head, a little confused by Ry's arms wrapped so tightly around his neck. "Thanks, Lug. You're welcome to join us tonight…"

"No, no. Glad we could help, and I've been meaning to check out those cars since that club started." He gave Calvin a knowing wink. "Cal and I both caught the fever. I want one, too. I'd better get along. I told Tabs I'd take her to the fireworks, so I'd best get my errands done." He glanced at Jaime and didn't frown, then smiled and waved at the boys. "Ya'll have fun."

Tad looked at his oldest son. "Have you been telling your brother stories, young man?"

Calvin looked a little embarrassed. "No."

"What makes him so convinced that a few days with your mom will be the end of the world?"

Calvin shrugged, but his dad's stern look had Jaime wanting to confess, even though she thought she was innocent. It worked on Cal.

"We don't wanna go with Mom." He reached over and took Jaime's hand and looked up at her. "We want you to be our mom. Mom's always busy, and we know you don't love us yet, but we're gonna keep trying. Don't make us go with the dragon lady."

Jaime felt like the weight of the world was resting on her shoulders. This was the thing she'd been striving to avoid; the confusing jumble of feelings. An angry father stepped in and saved her from having to answer.

"Young man, I'll not tolerate that language about your mother. I've warned you about staying out of grown-up business and…"

Cal cut him off defiantly while Ry watched from his perch. "You aren't trying hard enough, Dad. You stink at grown up business."

Jaime assumed the young man squeezing her hand had come to the end of his rope. Her dad would've walloped her for backtalk, but Tad's hard frown softened.

"You're right, son. I do stink at grown up business." He looked at Jaime. "The boys and I are gonna pass on the afternoon's activities and go back to the house." He came over and took Cal's hand from Jaime. "It sounds like we have some man business to discuss."

Jaime said, "Should I come? Seems I…"

"No, I don't think so, Jaime." His voice was tinged with sorrow, and she felt a lump form in her throat. "This is going to be a discussion about how we are going to get along just fine when you are on your way. Boys, let's go."

Calvin gave her a needy look, and Ryan just stared at her. He'd put his thumb in his mouth and he only did that when he was really upset. Grown up business, huh? What did she know about discussing grown up business, anyway?

Opting to avoid Tad all together, she cleaned up in one of the bathhouses and borrowed an outfit from Lana to watch the fireworks. She arrived alone at the ball field and found a semi private place to spread her blanket out where she was still likely to see the fireworks. She jumped to her feet when she saw her parents walking toward her.

Jaime looked from her mother to her father with total shock. Lug had been to the barbershop this afternoon and was wearing nice jeans and a collared shirt that fit him. Her mom was all made up and… wearing jeans? More importantly, to Jaime's experienced eye, they had both recently gotten laid, and the possessive arm Lug had around Tabby made it impossible not to figure out the details.

"As I was saying, Jasmine, your father has something to say to you." Tabby gave him a little nudge with her elbow, then slid her arm around his waist. Solidarity. Great. If it wasn't good news, she was in big trouble.

"Yes, sir?" Jaime heard the words, but wished she'd managed more disrespect. Heaven knows he's dished disrespect in spades.

"I…" He looked at Tabby, then back at Jaime. "I'm sorry I

didn't try harder to accept your career choices, Jaime. You were so much like me, I thought you'd follow in my footsteps, but you made your own choices, and for that I'm proud." He swallowed nervously, then said it again. "I'm proud of you."

Jaime sat down. Ten years. Ten years, her family had splintered because he wouldn't give her that one little thing. Her mother walks back into town, they bang the headboard a few times, and finally he's proud of her! What gives?

"Ah, shades," she muttered. "Lug… Dad. I'm… speechless."

"Well, that's a first," he said dryly, and Tabby elbowed him a bit more sharply. "But being bull-hea… uhm, strong willed and outspoken is what makes you who you are, daughter."

Jaime could feel tears in her eyes, and she couldn't allow it. She looked over his shoulder, aiming her gaze upward a bit. It was a trick she'd learned a long time ago to keep threatening tears from falling. It didn't work.

One, two, three freaking tears escaped, and somehow her dad's arms enfolded her awkwardly. Jaime didn't think he'd hugged her since she was about six when she realized if she acted more like her brother, like a boy, he was a lot less uncomfortable.

Somehow, she was bawling. Quick to bring her emotions into check, she sniffled and pulled back, wiping away her tears, much to her dad's clear relief.

"Uhm, so…" He put his hands on her shoulder. "So, your mom's going to be moving back in with me, and we'll want to see our grandsons as often as possible, okay? So go ahead and marry the boy and that'll be good."

Jaime's eyes narrowed at her dad just a little, but she didn't have it in her to get angry just now, and instead a chuckle escaped.

"Look, you two connivers. I know you're worried you're getting old, but you'll just have to work on Jake for grandkids. Tad and I aren't getting married." As she said it, she realized that meant Jake and Kat's kid, and the idea left her feeling a little funny. That was their problem, though.

Tabby just smiled serenely at her daughter and leaned into her husband. "We'll see, but don't worry. Now that I'm home, and I've got you and your father back, you can bet I'll be working on my son, the scoundrel."

Her smile said there was no hope for either her or her twin, and Jaime had to admit she was a little scared, but she wasn't about to get pushed around now. "Mom, are you wearing blue jeans… and cowboy boots?"

Tabby positively beamed. "I am. Your dad has been teaching me how to feed those bullies he has penned up in the backyard. I lifted a hay bale by myself."

Jaime glanced at her hands where her own calluses were building. "Yeah. That's actually kind of cool, isn't it? Tad has had me…" she trailed off, sensing a win in her mother's knowing smile.

"Well, unless you guys want to join me, I think the fireworks are about to start."

"We have a private place, too, over there." Her dad winked at her. She wasn't sure whether to be weirded out or laugh.

"Well, you loooovvebirds better settle in for the show."

The embarrassed flush that rose on her dad's cheeks was almost worth having cried on his shoulders. She hugged them both. Lug's hug was still stiff, but for the first time in forever, watching them walk off arm in arm, Jaime felt… forgiven.

When Tad and his kids showed up to watch the fireworks, he planned for them all to sit on the tailgate. They were all three wrung out and exhausted, and if he had any sense, he would have just put the boys to bed and fallen in beside them. The amount of angst stirred up in his kids was crushing.

Hydro hopped out of the truck as soon as they pulled into the parking lot and dashed towards a jasmine bush further out.

Tad rolled his eyes. His dog hadn't jumped out in months, and he recognized the little yellow VW as the likely reason for the abandonment now.

The boys looked at him as he shifted back into gear and pulled closer to where Jaime was parked. He wasn't forcing his dog away from her in front of everyone. Not that being caught parking in the corner with her was any better.

She called out. "I don't have any fried chicken, but I have a sweet view and a big dog on my lap. Ya'll might as well join us."

The boys grinned at each other and scrambled out of the truck. Like the last three hours of talking hadn't even happened.

The marriage conversation left this weird atmosphere that neither of them could shake. The bar had become way too tense, and he was glad it was over. It was a blast, but if he was going to let loose, he wanted it to be on the other side of the bar. He would be glad if he never had to hear someone ask for a light beer again.

"Hi," she told him shyly when he brought up the rear. She was wearing a cute little short set, and she had a bottle of bug spray she was already offering the boys.

"Hey, you sure you don't mind us crashing your spot? We missed the good pick since we got around late. Man business," he said, hopefully reminding the boys.

"Yeah, sure." She pushed the dog off her leg where he was practically laying on her and gestured to the other end of the blanket. The kids had flanked the girl and the dog.

Sheesh. A deep boom filled the sky, and Tad grabbed a seat with resignation. How was he supposed to pretend it wasn't tugging at him to be around her? They were done. No coming back from their last deep talk, and though they'd managed to work together the last two days, it had been insane. No room to catch a breath, let alone have a thought beyond the crowds.

He hadn't figured out what to do yet, but he knew something was bound to happen. At this point, they were going to end up in bed and kiss his principles goodbye. He'd have to love her once before she left, like that whole "love it and let it go" thing.

The fireworks were over and he'd barely seen them. Cal and Jaime were talking about their favorites, and Hydro and Ry were both laying across Jaime, mostly asleep. What had he done?

Chapter 14

The deal she made with Tad was killing her. His idea of early and hers was so far off, it wasn't fair. But he'd held up his end, so she wouldn't be the one to skimp. When her alarm went off again, she peered at the time and pulled herself out of bed and into her jeans.

Lana had given her a vintage kelly green tee with a fuzzy brown tractor and lettering that read, "A Roll in the Hay Makes My Day." It was her last day to haul hay, and she'd been dying to wear it. She pulled it on over a sports bra and grabbed the thin button-down Tad had given her. She stroked the soft shirt, then smelled it. Despite having washed it several times, it smelled like their mingled sweat. It was too many layers for this gross humidity, but she loved how well it protected her from hay scratches and bug bites. For now, she tied it around her waist.

They'd been working hay for three days now. The boys had gone with their mom for a few days, and Tad said the weather forecast was right for getting it all done.

There was a lull at the resort after the holiday—the recovery lull—and she felt comfortable leaving Kobi to run the show this week. She'd check on her daily, because they all needed a break, but it seemed hard work was a staple for anyone rooted here.

Tad had told her to drive the truck, and she thought he was giving her the simple job because he was lifting and stacking the square bales on to the flatbed trailer she was pulling. By the second day, he yelled at her so many times to slow down, speed up, drive straighter, and stay out of the lower fields if they looked boggy, that she'd jumped out and told him to drive the freaking thing himself. She'd stack hay.

He hadn't even commented, just switched positions. That was yesterday, and she prayed he would ask her to drive again today.

It had been pure torture. Her hands were so sore she didn't know if she'd be able to grab the twine strands that held the bales together. But she would pull on the deer hide gloves he'd given her and not say a word.

She left her cabin and headed to the barn where Mr. Wonderful was waiting, whistling some off-key country tune as he counted his cows, making sure everyone came up for breakfast.

He said he didn't have to feed them this time of year, just liked to keep them coming up, so he poured them out a delicious sorghum selling grain and the cows tried to kill each other for it.

They had one large field left to cut, rake, bale, haul, and stack into the steamy barn. Apparently, the rain had been good, and the hay was plentiful. She knew it was heavy… and infinite.

"Morning, sunshine."

His face lit up with delight, and if it weren't for his tendency to annoy her, she would have found it endearing…

"There's a sausage biscuit on the truck seat for you."

"Thanks," Jaime muttered, spying the coffee thermos and loving him a little more. By noon she'd be drinking more water than she could ever have imagined just to stay hydrated, but coffee was what she needed now, and it helped to improve her mood.

She had resisted breakfast the first day, and Tad had warned her she'd regret it. By lunch that day, she'd almost passed out stacking hay "just so" in the barn. She unwrapped the plastic around the homemade biscuit and started nibbling on sausage.

"So last run today, right? Then we're done?" Jaime asked, trying not to sound desperate.

"Done with hay for at least six weeks, then I think I might cut again if this growing keeps up. But you are off the hook for sure." He laughed. "You know you didn't have to see this through."

"We had a deal," she said. And she hadn't asked her dad to team up with Tad yet. But when the kids got home, she'd put a plan into play that would have the guys handling it themselves.

Tad finished his count, making a note on a clipboard hanging in the tool room, and came over to the pickup.

He looked so yummy, his ratty John Deere ball cap pulled low on his head. He looked better than a man should in jeans that were worn too thin. He wore a gray sleeveless shirt, seemingly oblivious to the scratchiness of the hay.

"I thought you said you had enough to feed through the winter already." Jaime looked at the full barn.

"Yep. I'm hoping to get another cutting. This stuff sells about three dollars a bale. If I can make enough to sell, I can upgrade to a round baler and make this work a little less manual. Are you ready? Daylights a burning."

Jaime rolled her eyes and climbed up in the passenger seat of the filthy pickup. "Might as well be. Why don't you just buy what you need? You have the money."

He gave her a look. "That would lessen the reward, wouldn't it?"

She scowled, but they fell into an easy rhythm, and Jaime drove. It seemed she must have learned a little cause he didn't yell at her once. He was lucky, because if he had, she'd also devised delightful ways to torture him when she got back in her own territory.

Tad lifted the last of his square bales off the truck bed and used his knee to buck it up toward the top of the mountain of squares. He looked over at Jaime, stretched out on the hard ground outside the barn, and smiled. She might argue the entire time, but the woman would work, and looked mighty fine doing it.

She opened one eye, pulling her hand wearily in place to shade her eyes from the late afternoon sun when she looked at him. "You swear that is the last load?"

"Til this fall. Yep." He stood back, admiring the full hay barn. His first. Ranching was filling his life with first times—mostly pleasant ones. This hay season had been hot and dry, perfect for the work, though the long hours sapped every bit of moisture from one's body.

If everything went as planned, next year he would have his equipment working for the round baler, but as it was, the 1200 bales they had stacked would feed his small herd through the next year. With the extra labor so generously provided by his temporary tenant, it was a win!

A feisty look crept over her face, and he saw intent. She stood up, a trifle unsteadily, and glanced down toward the riverbank, and back at him.

"I haven't seen any boats all day…"

"We did have those kayakers earlier, but yeah, it's been a slow day down there." She was not considering a float. She could barely stand.

She smiled innocently, and he knew something was up. "Look, I'm going to unhook the baler, and we can get out of here. The boys should be back this evening, and I want to get in a blessed shower."

She nodded thoughtfully. "I have another idea. Let's go swimming. Nothing sounds better than cool river water soaking the heat out of me."

He looked down at his jeans and boots.

"Hey, don't give me that. The first time I met you, you went swimming in your jeans. Besides, I'm okay with you taking them off."

As she turned and walked toward the river, she started unbuttoning the thin long sleeve shirt he'd lent her, and pulled off the t-shirt with the tempting innuendo.

Continuing toward the water in a sports bra and jeans, his

shirt thrown over her shoulder, he watched as she stripped down to her barely there underwear and slipped into the water. After dunking under, she surfaced and looked up the hill, where he felt frozen in place.

"C'mon, this feels amazing. I can see you have boxers on, and your virtue might be safe."

The way she unabashedly expressed herself tempted a man.

He quickly splashed in the icy water with a sigh of content. Wearing his boxers. He did not want to be caught skinny dipping in broad daylight at this play in the game.

"I don't know what it is about you, Jasmine. Your sensuality stirs me."

He sent a small splash in her direction, and she rewarded him with the smile of pure pleasure that drove him crazy. She had nine smiles he'd been able to count, and this was a rare one. Happiness.

When did he turn into a romantic fool?

"I was so set to dislike you." Her eyes were deep pools of bright aqua he could swim into and languish in forever. Her mouth begged him, as it had since that first day, to be kissed, possessed.

"Must you call me that?" Jaime asked softly. "No one calls me Jasmine except my persistent mother. That girl was a different girl."

"I think maybe you're the same girl inside and you use these rough textures to keep the idiots away."

She grinned at him, and her closeness had his pulse skittering like a randy teenager. Did she have to smell so sweet? She should stink. He knew he did. It was a torture to not be able to taste all of her, to hold her tight and love her all afternoon.

"It didn't work so well with you, ya idiot. I warned you about me. I'm not a nice girl." She said it like she didn't want to believe it, but she did. "I've been covering my rear so long… I don't let people get too close."

Tad's arms had slipped around her and she was pressing her sumptuous curves against him. "We're pretty close now…"

She nodded, not breaking eye contact with him.

"But this is sexual, not real."

He felt like she'd dunked him. He stiffened, but didn't let her go. Despite his defensive reaction, he had to admit he didn't want to let her go because he had been imagining how very little work it would take to get her naked.

"Does everything have to be so black and white with you?" Tad asked.

"Yes." She sighed, resting her head against his shoulder. "It's self-preservation."

"I'd be lying if I said I could handle you, but how am I supposed to just let you self-preserve your way out of my life?"

"I don't know what we're doing here, Tad. We laid out clear, sensible lines and we just keep kicking the dirt over them."

She pulled back out of his arms, then dunked her head under the water for a long few seconds. When she came back up, he felt like she might be close to tears.

"You're right, and I don't think it's because we both didn't have the best intentions. You have, what, 5 or 6 weeks left?"

"Yeah," she muttered. "A lot of work to do in a short time."

"So, let's just let this play out like a summer romance should. We enjoy it, maybe a little kissing and stuff when the boys aren't around. They will never forgive me if I don't at least ask you to be my girlfriend. I don't care about what my lawyer said. That was a stupid reason to propose, and I regret it. I don't want to live my life to suit other people anymore, other than my shorties, anyway. I want you and I can see you'll be happier when you leave, so we break it off then. And you go."

She was staring at him with glossy eyes, and he knew he should shut up.

"Let's just enjoy the rest of the summer? The boys are already begging to help Lug with the reunion, so even though we aren't going to be rubbing elbows behind the bar, we're still going to be stuck up in each other's grills until you're done here. I don't know how much more temptation my libido can take. Will you say something already?"

"I'm thinking." She shook her head. "Tad, babe, no offense here, but how could that even work? I couldn't possibly be the mother those boys need, even in the short term. I'm not a kid person."

He laughed at her.

"What?" Jaime asked, irritated.

"You? Not a kid person?" He scoffed. "You talk to every kid you meet, and they can't wait to hang out with you as if you're their new best friend. I might mention you also have the same effect on men and dogs. It's a little annoying."

She splashed around a little, frolicking in the cold clean water running past her delicious curves.

"That's just my charming personality, babe. What about your charm?" She splashed at him. "I haven't exactly noticed people running the other direction when you flash that innocent-looking grin in their direction. Especially women."

"Hasn't worked too well with you."

She shook her head. "You haven't even tried to charm me. You've treated me with hostility or kid gloves so far. When I glimpse the real you behind your shields. I wonder how you have everyone fooled so handily?"

"You should talk, Jasmine." Her truth pricked him deep, but it was a dual issue. "You're the queen of pretend."

"Well, royalty, anyway. Look…" she glanced up at the sun, judging the passing of time like she'd lived here all her life… "Never mind. I'm beat. This was perfect, but let's head home."

She shifted around to leave, not even noticing the pleasure she'd lit in him when she'd called his ranch home.

"Not so fast, buttercup."

She stopped before he got the full view of her walking away wet again.

"I think we need the release."

She hesitated. "If a little kissing and stuff happens over the next few weeks, so it does. I won't deny I like it. I want it. But it breaks the rules I have in place to keep people from being hurt. You're a big boy, I think you can take it. I can take it, but I can already tell it won't feel as good as I thought it would when I leave here. But I am leaving. This place isn't for me. I have a job offer I'm planning to take this winter."

She stepped out of the water and put his shirt on. Despite her tone, all he wanted to do was take her out of it and taste her.

"So where does that leave us big kids, then?" He asked instead.

She shook her head, exasperated, then flashed him her "I'm up for anything" grin. "If we can keep the kids and my parents' expectations in check, I'm down with a little kissing on the sly."

Later that night, after Tad tucked in Cal and Ry, he stepped out on to the back porch to have a beer and found Jaime sitting there, already drinking one. He reached into the cooler, fetching a can.

"I helped myself."

Her sultry voice floated on the wind and Tad considered how many times today he wished he'd made love to her instead of taking the high road.

"I see that. You seem comfortable on my porch, but not so much inside. What's up with that?"

He settled himself against the porch railing so he could watch her chilling on his swing in the moonlight. Her hair flowed over her bare shoulders with wild abandon, the snaky curls driving Tad crazy with lust to bury his face in them… in her. She was alluring.

"Just don't want to get too comfortable," she mumbled. "I think we need to talk some more." She pulled one foot up under her leg and gave a little push with the other one, the motion from the swing gently stirring the still air on the porch.

"Hmm. I think… I think we should talk later. Do you want to make out?"

He startled a laugh out of her, and the serious and pained expression left her lovely features. "You stole my line," she said. "Maybe later, handsome. My folks have some ideas, and they're worrying me…"

He talked her down, hand in hand. These next weeks would be a challenge on several levels, but he'd enjoy it before it hurt, and help the boys toughen up to take it, too. She was worth it.

Chapter 15

The morning started off overcast, but it was supposed to be blue skies later in the day. She needed them to improve her mood. She hoped she'd made a good call, agreeing to go to her parents for dinner tonight. With Tad. And his kids. Man.

If she could even survive that long. There was a council meeting early in the day to work on the reunion. Then she had an interview with another bartender, because she had a feeling Kobi wanted more kitchen hours. Then she'd prep schedules for the next two weeks. Hopefully. Then dinner and a show.

First, the council meeting to work on the reunion. Goody.

Unfortunately, her mood matched the sky.

There was a knock at the door, and Jaime answered it, hoping it was Tad so she could vent her frustration on him. She got lucky.

"I'm hoping this is a conjugal visit. I could sure use some of that release you were talking about."

A pained look crossed his face. "I wish, but I'm on a mission." He stepped inside. "But I have time to kiss you soundly." He did, and he left her breathless. Her mood improved markedly.

"No, look, I was wondering… we can see you're working your tail off on the reunion deal and I was wondering, well, Cal and Ry were wondering, if you can use some extra hands. The boys love your dad and they are getting pretty fired up by the stories he's been telling. So, I guess I'm officially asking if we can all help."

Jaime's mouth dropped open in surprise. "So, have we won you over, then? All in for Falls Mill Resort?"

"If I can manage the logistics, I might even strike up a little deal with Garrett to do some guided floats. Lana mentioned you wanted me to do one the day of the reunion and it got me thinking. Maybe I don't have to wait for the boys to get older. If I just did special events, it would round out my livelihood nicely. So, I guess I'm all in."

She clutched her chest, miming shock. "I never thought to see the day, my friend."

He winced.

Man, she was stomping all over him, and after he kissed her so nicely.

"Yeah, well, I've got to go. T-ball practice today. I thought I might ask your dad if he wanted to go on a camping trip with us guys this weekend. I bet it would be okay if you and your mom came."

She gave him a look of horror. "Surely you jest?"

"Food for thought. It's just the boys have been pestering me to ask, and after yesterday, I thought maybe—"

"Sure, no, right," Jaime said as she stepped out onto the step and waved at the boys loading up in the truck. "Look, I'll think of agreeable tasks for each of you willing fellows. I can use all the help I can get."

When she pulled in at the restaurant when they were supposed to meet, her heart sank. Kat was waiting for her, leaning up against a car, and looking like a million bucks.

"Jaime. I'd heard you finally blessed Riverbend Falls with your presence."

"Kat." Jaime's heart twisted up. Best friend and betrayer. "Just doing Lana a favor. I'm not getting comfortable."

"You look pretty comfortable to me. You're running the show for the reunion and... are you shacking up with Tad?"

Jaime felt a wave of heat rush to her face. "Where have you been, anyway?"

"I had some things to take care of." Kat shook her head impatiently, as if she didn't want to talk about it.

"With Jake?" Jaime pressed.

"It's been ten years since you asked me what I've been up to. Why start now?"

"Kat, that's not fair. You guys left first, without saying goodbye."

"You ruined our wedding announcement by getting us arrested with weed. Eloping was a way to dodge the judgmental glares of our elders. And not have to deal with you. I admit."

"Deal with me?" Jaime's heart felt ripped from her chest. "He's my twin. You were my best friend. Would it have been too much of a hardship to include me in your plans?"

"I see age hasn't tempered your selfish nature." Kat gave her a pitying look. "If you've paid any attention to what was going on outside your world, you'll remember we have issues I'd rather not talk about. And I wasn't planning to share my personal life."

"Really? I find it hard to believe you'd miss a chance to put me in my place, so if not that, why are you here?" Jaime was impatient to end this. Seemed like she missed them way more than they missed her. Old news now, anyway. "So why would I give a fig for what you and your sweetheart are doing?" She shook her head and started to walk past Kat.

"Oh, come up for air, Jaime. We split last year."

"What?" Jaime asked with disbelief. They were inseparable.

"I'm not here to catch you up. Grandpa Eli's excited about the reunion, and I promised him I'd see what I could do to help. Imagine my surprise when I get home, and I'm told to ask you. I didn't see that coming."

"Kat, I'm sorry." Jaime didn't want them to be having problems. She just wished they'd taken a little time for her… she wasn't used to being left out, and it had hurt.

"Save it." Kat said. "I shouldn't have come." She turned to go, but Jaime caught her arm. She wasn't that girl anymore.

"Wait a minute. I am selfish, then and now. I rarely apologize for it, but you and Lan were sisters to me, and I owe you more. I regret what I did back then, and I can't change it, but I am a better friend now."

Kat looked at her skeptically, and Jaime laughed. "I know. That was out of character, right? So will you forgive me for getting us arrested and ruining your wedding plans, and not picking up the phone and telling you this sooner?"

Kat threw her head back and let out a deep, throaty laugh.

"I forgive you for those three things. We'll start there. In the meantime, do you have a plan for in there?" She nodded her head in the porch's direction, where a few ladies were hovering, the smell of intrigue in the air, trying to see any hugs, sparks, or maybe even a good old-fashioned fistfight. Hopes were high.

"I was going to lay out my ideas and try to hold my ground." Jaime felt fear, and she worried the mavens would sense it.

"For Grandpa Eli, I'll back you up and try to help. If you want my help?"

Jaime felt a flood of relief. Lana should be there, but she'd already sold Jaime down the river. Kat was unlikely to try to force Jaime to stay. Clearly, Jaime needed to think about what else she needed to ask forgiveness for.

They joined the half dozen matrons that ruled the town, and the lovely elite Cynthia. Finally, Lana arrived, and Jaime had a glimmer of hope that the three might hold their own. Barely.

Ms. Goodwin eyed Jaime with interest. She didn't like being under the old lady's thumb, but it seemed it had happened. Only this time, Jaime knew she was being sized up as more than an onerous teenager.

The women in this town had decided to marry her and Tad off, and everybody's favorite wonder boy should have nothing but the best. She was doomed to be a disappointment, but it was what it was.

She sighed, passing the lists back to Mrs. Bunsen, the sweet little jewelry store owner from main street.

"Lists, lists, lists. How can you guys get anything done for writing all the time?" She tapped her brain. "That's what this is for. Anyway, with about two exceptions, that's all done. We've got this, ladies! I need actual physical bodies before the event, but today's meeting has provided us with an exceptional list of volunteers. I'll get to work on the job assignments."

"Speaking of lists," Lana asked, "do you have a final reservation count yet?"

"It's still growing. I've heard positive response from at least two-thirds of Lug's remaining regiment and they all want to come and bring family. There's almost two hundred people confirmed…" Jaime shuffled down to a particular page, "and I am still waiting to hear from roughly thirty more people. I think this is going to be a memorable event! Has Garrett stopped fussing over the menu yet?"

Lana smiled at Emily, Garrett's grandma. "Nah, he's still working on ways to make it more special, but I've warned him about the volume, so let's hope he doesn't get too over the top. You know us, though. We want everything to be just right."

Jaime smiled, and turned the meeting over to Emily, Garrett's grandma, who was coordinating the desserts.

Lana leaned over and whispered to Jaime. "I'm serious. I can't thank you enough. I was sure you would buck this job since we railroaded you. Maybe to spite Lug. I never dreamed you'd work so hard at it."

"The free publicity is worth the hassle of getting pushed around." She narrowed her eyes at her friend, whispering back. "You were sneaky, though. My dad's really into this, so that helps. I'd have to be a real jerk not to want to help."

"I wouldn't say jerk, but it's tough to budge you once you decide, Jaime." Lana grinned at Kat, and it felt like old times.

Kat lounged back in her chair, doodling on a napkin, glancing in solidarity with them every so often, while the ladies went through the motions of closing the meeting. They would have one more in a few weeks, then it would be done. It seemed like a really short time away.

"Which two things?" Ms. Goodwin grabbed her cane, pushing out of the cozy restaurant chair. "The day I entrust the good name of this town to a bunch of upstarts without keeping tabs on what they're doing, well, that'll be the day I get old." She glared at Jaime, begging her to argue, but Jaime just smiled.

"Of course, Ms. Goodwin. I'd be honored if you let me provide you with a seat of honor during the proceedings, since you had such a big part in the war."

"Darn right, I did. Somebody had to patch up the returning soldiers, and it couldn't be someone with a weak constitution. Lord knows I'm a tough old bird." She strode to the door after the last of the party and stopped to shake her cane at Jaime, "I know you girls have been at odds, so I'm not sure what's going on with you two, but don't think you can fool old Lenore. You girls make up and play nice."

"She sure hasn't changed in all these years, has she?" Jaime looked after the old woman fondly and glanced at Lana and Kat. The three together again. It felt… good.

"She liked that bit about the special seating. Your powers of persuasion never fail to amaze me, J." Lana stood. "If you girls are done with me, I have to get back to the clubhouse."

The girls hugged, and it seemed to Jaime that something special had happened. Jaime gave Kat a shrewd look after Lana left. "You've got something big going on, I can tell. Want to sign up for floral arrangements for the grandstand? Your garden is just freaking bursting with flowers—I noticed on a drive by— so I'm assuming you might like that job? I've got an interview to do and one more challenge to take on before the day is over. Are we good?"

Kat nodded thoughtfully, and Jaime knew she was already selecting flowers as she got ready to leave with the grace of a heroine in an old silent movie. "It's a start."

"I'm glad, Kat. I've missed you."

Surprised, Kat gave Jaime a guarded look. "I'm not expecting us to be besties again. I'm just here if you need me."

"Well, Kat, we were friends before. Maybe it'll work out again. Who knows? Lunch soon? Test run?" She hoped Kat took her up on the offer. She wouldn't admit it out loud, but her life wasn't the same without Kat in it. They could never go back, of course, but what if there was a future?

She'd never met any other friends she related to so well…
though she was finding Tad terribly relatable lately.

"Sure. In the meantime, let me know if you need any help.
It's really important to Eli. I'll be in and out of pocket for the
rest of the summer, but I'm here for you." With a swish of long
silky black hair, Kat was gone, and Jaime had work to do. The
stakes had just gone up.

This could be a disaster on so many levels.

"Hi Mom." Reaching across the threshold for a hug, her
affectionate mother barely had eyes for her.

"Calvin, Ryan, you boys are handsome little devils, aren't
you? C'mon in here. Jaime, Tad, make yourselves comfortable
in the living room. Dinner will be in about thirty minutes." Her
blue eyes sparkled brightly and Jaime sensed some kind of
mischief afoot. "Boys, come with me. Lug and I have a little
surprise for you guys."

Though slightly bewildered, probably by the crazy hues of
her mother's broomstick skirt, the boys followed her down the
hall, walking very close together. Jaime sat in the armchair,
pointedly not joining Tad on the couch. The only reason she
was going through with this meal was because she had an idea
itching at her, and when Jaime saw a chance to fix something,
the need to take care of it would nag at her until she at least
tried.

Lug strolled in, still sober, and glanced at them both as he
sat across from Tad. He crossed his legs comfortably, an amber
liquid sloshing in the highball in his hand. "My boy. How's the
ranching going?"

Perfect, Dad! He couldn't have made this any easier on her.
Tad shrugged good-naturedly. It was about the same as always,
but Jaime took advantage of his hesitation to bait her dad.

"You wouldn't believe the down time he's suffering because
he can't keep his tractors running. He's terrible at maintenance."

Jaime gave Tad a silly smile, like she hadn't just offended him
for no reason. He wasn't bad with his hands, but with
mechanics, he just wasn't as strong—and it was costing him

time and money.

Tad needed someone he could trust to help. He just glared at her, his mustache twitching. Jaime felt confident she wouldn't have to say another word. A quick glance at Lug confirmed it.

His bushy white eyebrows were knit in concentration, and Jaime could hear him estimating as he figured out how he wanted to conduct his horse trading. Her dad loved to barter.

"You've got that Old Golden jubilee, don't ya? The '53 special?"

Tad switched his attention to Lug with a final searing look that promised retribution.

"Yeah. It was my dad's, and he used to drive it in parades, but I haven't been able to get it running. I swear, it's always something. I have a weary 1980 Ford tractor that gets the job done. I'd sure like to rake with the Jubilee, though. Preventative maintenance is killing me. I'm always just a little behind schedule. It works out something new needs fixed before I get around to preventing the breakdowns." He shrugged. "Just the nature of the beast, though."

"Well, I'd like a crack at the Jubilee. I don't suppose that orange beast out back caught your attention. It's a bit big for my operation, but I sure like driving it. I've been eyeing your cattle. You spent a pretty penny on that herd. Ever think you could have just bought one new tractor and maybe less quality hides?"

"It might have been wiser, in hindsight." Tad leaned back on the couch, settling in for guy talk. "Especially after I saw the new Kubotas at the county fair this past year. Tricked out. But I decided good quality cattle were going to be a factor when I chose to be a rancher, so that's where I started."

"I like your way of thinking. I think we might help each other out. See, turns out they didn't call me Colonel Lugwrench in the Army for nothing. I used to maintain all the big rigs around there, and I tell ya, I've worked on about every kind of diesel engine you can think of. Why don't we see about working on some trades? Maybe some labor for a calf each year. It is a fine herd you're building…"

Watching her dad and Tad talk, she realized they'd forgotten she was in the room. Ah, misdirection was a beautiful thing. It would only take twenty minutes or so for them to figure it out.

She went to see what her mom was up to with the boys.

She wandered down the long hallway, her mind cluttered with memories of her and her Jake racing down these halls. When they had moved to Riverbend Falls, it had felt to Jaime like the first time they ever stopped long enough to be a family.

She could see the indent just below eye level where she and Jake had been practicing bunting in the hallway. Jaime got carried away and smashed a huge hole in the wall. Jake tried to help her fix it, but they ended up moving all the furniture so it wouldn't look weird, and they moved a bookcase into the hallway. Lug got torqued that they moved his recliner in the living room during the process and ordered them to put everything back.

Then he saw the hole. When he realized she'd been practicing batting, he'd softened up and tweaked her baseball hat. "I knew you were gonna be a real slugger. Next time, Jaime, outside. Now, help me fix this properly before your mother sees it."

She stopped at her old bedroom door, closed up tight. Out of curiosity, she opened it and stared in morbid fascination. It looked exactly as it had when she left, down to the baseball cards stacked on the center of her desk with her goodbye note still resting on it.

Although it was unhealthy, surely, she was shocked to find that her presence had not been erased. Had Jake been home or was his room also a captured moment in time? She pulled the door shut and walked on. Her dad had closed the betrayal out. So could she. She would ask her dad about giving the baseball cards to Cal and Ry.

He was the only one who called her Jaime then. She'd always thought Jasmine was too elegant for a tomboy like herself, but back then, her nickname had been her thing with her dad. He was always more relaxed with her when he forgot she was a girl, and he had so much to teach.

Her musings were interrupted by yelling from Jake's old

room. Ry was shouting. "Get him, Mrs. Tab! Cream him." Her mom's urgent cries and Cal's silence had Jaime hurrying the rest of the way, a little freaked out. The scene shocked her.

Her brother's old room was a video game den and her mom and Cal were battling out a car racing game. The look on her mom's face had her bursting into laughter, and her mom glanced at her with chagrin when Cal let out a triumphant whoop.

"You distracted me," Tabby complained. "I was winning."

"You were not, Mrs. Tab. Cal had you the whole time. Can I play next?" Ryan was hopping around with effervescent energy.

Her mom stood up gracefully from the floor. "I've got to check on dinner. You guys can play one more game, then wash your hands where I showed you and meet us at the table. You boys were challenging opponents. I'll be practicing."

The boys giggled, returning to the game. Jaime followed her mom into the kitchen. "Is that straight out bribery, Mom?"

Tabby smiled at her innocently. "I heard through the grapevine you might need an occasional sitter for the boys. Surely you weren't thinking anyone else would spoil them the way your dad and I will." She pulled a sumptuous looking roast out of the oven, and Jaime's stomach lurched hungrily at the sight of it. Her mom chuckled, also pulling a tray of chicken nuggets off the lower rack. "So how long until I can insist they call me Grandma?"

Tad entered the kitchen, cocking his eyebrow at Jaime, and she prayed he had not heard her mom. Good grief.

"Tabby, something smells like heaven in here." He wrinkled his nose in amusement at the nuggets. "I see you did your research. I'm not sure I'll ever be able to convince Ry and Cal to come home with me tonight. They're already asking to spend the night with Lug, and he doesn't seem to help me to discourage them. Is there anything I can do to help?"

Her dad bellowed from behind them. "Don't be silly, my boy, that's women's work." He winked at Tabby and she raised her wooden spoon in mock attack, causing another outbreak of giggling from the boys who were clambering into chairs at the table.

"Don't let Lug fool you, boys. He was in the kitchen this morning at dawn working on his apple pie dumpling specialty. I just do the meats, and he does the sweets."

"She gives away my secrets. Well, boys, shall we work our way through this good grub so we can try my pie?"

"Yes please, I'm starved," Cal said, hungrily eyeing the spread. "Could you please pass the nuggets, Mrs. Tabs?"

With a knowing grin at Jaime, her mom said, "Certainly, young man. Did your dad teach you such delightful manners?"

"No ma'am. He just taught me to be polite, especially to old folks."

Tad blushed heavily. "Calvin. That's your elders. You're supposed to be polite, especially to your elders."

"Yes sir," he said, heaping the provided macaroni and cheese next to his heaping pile of chicken nuggets. He turned back to her mom. "I meant to say, polite to the elderly."

Tad just shook his head. "We'll work on that," he muttered, as he sampled the roast. "This is the stuff dreams are made of, Tabby. I know where Jaime got her skills."

Despite the mounting tension from her folks' poorly veiled hints that Tad and Jaime get their act together, the rest of the evening went off without a hitch. Dad's apple dumpling pie was every bit as good as Jaime's childhood memories. Her dad had hardly ever been home, but the kids knew when he was, he would make stuff that pleased every sweet tooth, and it seemed he hadn't let old habits die.

Dueling, soft snores resonated from between them as Tad bumped down Old River road toward the ranch. The moon was full again, and Jaime would be gone after the next one.

She glanced at Tad's silhouette in the soft dash lights. How could she ever replace the laughter and joy that these three had brought into her life? Could she stay? She'd just slow her roll and see how things played out. That always worked before.

Chapter 16

"Are you going to come camping with us, Miss Jaime? Dad said girl scouts know all kinds of cool stuff to do at camp."

She was sitting at the table having lunch with what she was just now affectionately referring to as "the boys," easily including Tad and his sometimes-boyish behaviors on the same level as his young sons.

"Not this time, Cal. I have several things to take care of at the restaurant this week. Maybe next time," she said offhandedly, then hesitated a bit when Tad raised that inquisitive eyebrow at her and she flushed a little. "Well, maybe next time if you go again before Labor Day."

The sweltering summer heat seemed to saturate Tad's house, and even the typical light breeze that usually circulated through was not present.

"Are you boys going to catch some fish for dinner?"

"Yep," said Ry. "Dad says we have to catch fishes or we don't get supper. Are you good at catching fish?"

Jaime chuckled. "Not so much, but I can cook fish so many ways your head would spin."

She giggled when Ry started doing neck rolls kind of wildly, then he paused. "Dad, can you cook fish even one good way?"

Tad looked at his son with humor glinting in his grey-green

eyes, but he kept a straight face. "Don't you guys like raw fish? We could eat sushi like bears."

"Ooh gross!" Cal made a gagging noise. "Mom likes swushi, and she made us taste it and I threw up. It was bad. But if Jaime could cook it for us, I know I'd like it."

Tad grinned at Jaime. "People can't stop raving about your cooking, darlin'."

"Yeah, yeah, I get that a lot." She looked at the boys, then at Tad. "I tell you what, boys. If your dad tries to starve you, I want you to use my secret campfire recipe for not starving."

She dropped her partially eaten sandwich on her plate and, eyeing the banana bunch on the counter, she riffled through the cupboards.

"Hmmm, yeah… okay here we go, yep…" and eyeballing the supplies Tad had already packed in a tub, she snitched out the marshmallows and aluminum foil and came back to the table carrying the haul.

"What's all that?" Ry asked with wonder in his voice.

She set down bananas, peanut butter, a bag of leftover chocolate chips, raisins, and marshmallows.

"Well, boys, this is what we call banana boats. Now if you're starving, or better yet, you catch a bunch of fish and have a grand dinner, but your sweet tooth is still hungry, I want you to show your dad how to make these banana boats."

"Okay," said Ry. "Dad, close your eyes and don't listen so you don't hear the special recipe."

"Well son, how about if I clean up after lunch while you guys memorize the secret formula?"

"Okay, just don't listen." Cal and Ry got up and moved closer. The merriment in Tad's eyes was priceless, and Jaime lowered her voice to add to the mystery.

"Do you boys both have your pocket knives?" She eyed them, knowing Tad had been teaching them both how to "whittle" wood, and they had special instructions to always carry them carefully. Both boys nodded solemnly, and Jaime picked up a banana. "Okay, the most important thing to remember is we leave the skin on for this recipe."

Ry wrinkled his nose and eyed her dubiously. "You're always 'posed to take the peel off."

"Trust me here, kiddo. Okay, so you lay out a piece of foil for a table, enough to wrap all the way around the banana. Then carefully, with the peel still on," she wiggled her eyebrows at Ry, "cut a long slice in the banana. Then push the ends of the banana together just a little and it will look like a canoe. Then I want you to spoon peanut butter into the cavity you made—"

"Will this give us cavities? I don't like the dentist," Cal said.

Darn, they were cute.

"Not if you brush your teeth afterward," she said, and they both nodded as if they knew that already. "Besides, it's not that kind of cavity. It's more like a cave you're making in the banana," she said, and when they nodded, she continued. "Okay, so in the banana cave, spoon in some peanut butter, then sprinkle on marshmallows, raisins, chocolate chips… make them with whatever you like, okay?" They nodded again. "Now, take your tin foil table and wrap it around the banana and cinch the ends carefully so none of the good stuff spills out while you're cooking it."

"Cooking it?" Ry asked, wide eyed.

"Yep, then you set these down on the grill top for about ten minutes, then unwrap and cool. But don't cool them too much. They are gooey yummy, especially still warm."

"Can we try one now?" Ry reached over and fingered the chocolate chips wishfully.

"There's no fire, dummy," Cal said.

"Hey, no name calling," Jaime interjected. "But you will have to wait for the campfire. I've done my duty now, fellows. Even though I can't cook your fish, I won't worry about you all starving out there in the wilderness." She smiled and collected the supplies and dumped them in with the food Tad had packed. He was grinning at her again, and Jaime almost wished she could go with them. His smile warmed her down to her freakin toes, making her feel green as a schoolgirl. Maybe she would go.

"You make everything look good," he said under his breath. "I want a banana boat now."

She swatted at his arm and walked back to the table. "Look, I can't resist. I'll be late, but I'll be there. Guys, give me fives."

As she scored high-fives from each of them and a sly leer from Tad, she said, "I've got to go. Duty calls."

Mrs. Goodwin had surprised her with her grudging vocal support, but with Lana and Garrett paving the way, there was some definite relaxing happening around here. Mills Fall Bar and Grill was adding value to the community, people who wanted to work here.

She rounded out Kobi's schedule, and she put Zack on days in the kitchen, but she was glad Garrett had been willing to let her find someone else who could help work the restaurant on the weekends.

Garrett, bless his heart, just didn't have the time. She honestly thought he would do better making the Friday and Saturday night bar food for a few hours. He could hobnob in between orders and get a more realistic payback for his time.

She'd pitched the idea, and he went for it, glad to hand the dining room cooking over to the feisty chef she'd hired. He was from Louisiana, and she'd worked with him before. She knew he and Garrett would hit it off, so she called him, and he'd come.

Kobi moved in beside him on the line, planning to come back after she graduated. She shared hours upstairs and downstairs with Zack, who seemed on the straight and narrow for now. It was coming together, but Garrett was nervous about how much time he would have for anything once the baby came.

Their little one was expected in November, and they'd just found out she was a girl.

Jaime would be gone by then. Why had she jumped in if she couldn't fix it?

She'd had this concept of Riverbend Falls as an unfriendly place for the last decade, and it was a struggle to get rid of the stereotype, but some days it didn't feel unfriendly anymore.

She hung the schedule with a flourish on the icemaker and gathered her things to head home. She'd been putting off that last big task of the day because she dreaded scheduling her own name into the short jobs, but she knew someone had to do it. But after that she was done making them every two weeks.

As she turned out the lights and headed across the parking lot under the twinkling stars, Jaime looked back at the newly remodeled restaurant with a sense of wonder. If you had suggested to Jaime her best friend's hangout from childhood would be a tourist spot one day, she would've burst out laughing.

Yet, here she was, a grown woman, on the banks of Riverbend Falls, doing the job she'd trained for. Life had a way of surprising you with its unpredictable twists. Mrs. Rosati and the hens had adopted her somehow—even Ms. Goodwin, who'd threatened to switch her and twist her ear off.

These women had become, in the space of a few months, some of the Mill's best customers and they'd taken Jaime in as if she were a goose who'd just joined the flock.

No worries, just slide in here, next to me. They were so nice.

She flipped on her headlights to make the short drive back to Tad's ranch, knowing what alarmed her was the downright niceness of it all. Jaime had been feeling the same restlessness she always did, only this time it had an unfamiliar edge to it. She had a powerful urge to stay, and that scared her.

The light was on at the ranch house when Jaimie pulled in, and she could see Tad on the steps watching the wild antics in the front yard. Even though it was well after eight, the boys were running around the yard with jars full of lightning bugs, and Hydro, the big oaf, was running and snapping his jaws toward the bugs, as if he were urging someone to catch one for him.

She could see Tad rise to meet her when she pulled in, and knew this was what she was worried about. Three months ago, he'd refused to shake her hand when she'd introduced herself.

Now, here she was, pulling in on a scene from sitcomville, and Mister Consideration was waiting for her. He'd probably even saved her a plate of dinner. Jaime felt her emotions bubbling up, and it made her want to lash out at him.

He loped toward the car like an eager schoolboy, and her more feisty urges appreciated the view. He was a good-looking man, no doubt there. He pulled open her car door for her, just as she was getting ready to step out. How annoying.

"Hey there, worker chick. We saved ya a plate of supper. Do you want to eat on the porch? The boys talked me into waiting for you to get home, and your folks are meeting us at camp."

"No, I'm not hungry. I could use a beer." How frustrating it was to want him, to want to eat him up, but not want to hurt his feelings. She needed bright lights and parties, and instead she was going camping with her parents.

"Great, I'll grab you a beer. The boys have been playing pretty hard today, and they are excited. I honestly don't know how long they'll be awake for night fishing, but they want to try it. Good day?"

She stared at him, deciding quickly. "Fine. I'll change and grab an overnight bag. Then we'll go." The dog arrived to greet her, and with a quick wave at Cal and Ry, who were still engrossed in the glowing bugs, she invited the big dog to go with her as she went to the cabin to change and grab her stuff.

It was too much, Tad thought as he walked back toward the campfire light from the riverbank. He needed to walk for a minute and question his sanity. He'd arranged this camp out initially to get the boys out of the house. Then, he thought of taking Lug because the old man really loved his kids, and they had plenty to talk about. Then he stuck his foot in it and invited Jaime.

He was glad she came, even though she was uber cranky, but man... it defeated the purpose. To get away from her. Their "Jaime days" were coming to a close, and it was time to disentangle their lives. So, he brought her on a family camp trip.

And all he could think about was that she was going to get away before he showed her how much he loved her. And wasn't that a kicker? He had it bad. It smacked him in the face like a tequila hangover.

He loved her, without a doubt. So, he'd let her go. She was

a wild thing, and he dare not cage her.

Her parents had come early and set up camp so the boys could wait for Jaime. That hadn't been his plan either, but he'd gone along with it.

There was one other plan he hadn't gone along with, and it frustrated him. She wouldn't refuse, but it might hurt them both. He could tell she cared, but she was so dismissive of her own needs she'd never see it.

But he wanted her, at least once. Preferably not in his bed, where her memory would linger long after she was gone, but just once, he needed to show her how he felt.

"Care if I join you?"

His warm voice came from the shadows just a moment before the man appeared and fished a few beers from his cooler. She thought she would have turned him away, but she had just been wishing she'd grabbed a six-pack to bring.

"Sure. But I need to walk a little. If we run into a bear or something, I can run faster than you, so I would appreciate your company."

He fell in step with her and his warm presence fused into her soul, and she knew she was in real trouble. She was desperate to hear his rich laughter, his voice when it filled with desire, and that look of amused dissatisfaction that he wore so well.

She was falling in love. They walked without words for a few minutes toward the river, up a bit from where her folks had put in a johnboat anchored off the bank for fishing. She could hear their voices though, carrying down the water, and the sounds of the whippoorwills calling in the night nearly drowned out the jug-a-rum of the frogs calling for mates.

She popped the cap off her beer and took a long pull.

"That was a little much," Tad said. He grabbed a flashlight from his pocket and shined it around on the ground near a big, flat rock, which was partly covered by an overhead canopy of trees, lit up by the moonlight's soft embrace. He walked over and sat down.

Her heartbeat picked up. He was sending off some steady

vibes that mixed lust with dissatisfaction, and she wasn't entirely how to handle him.

"I was sure your mom was about to grab us by the ears and whisk us off to Vegas. She's not shy, is she?"

"No." Jaime laughed. Her mom was a whirlwind of chaos, and around her rainbows could shine while thunder struck. "My Mom's always been a driving force. Jake and I couldn't wait to get out on our own. Dad was so strict and Mom so easy going. It was like a miniature war zone to stay out of trouble. One thing, though, both are single-minded when they take a notion to do something."

It looked like a pleasant spot, so she sat and took a swallow off her beer, and fished out her vape and took a few drags guiltily. "I try not to vape in front of the kids. I am a bad example walking, so I curb it where I can."

She gave a weak grin, but he wasn't having any. "You sure are hard on yourself," Tad murmured, his voice blending smoothly with the night sounds to cover her in a gentle calm.

"I think we have to talk about some things, Tad." Since the boys would be gone at least an hour checking jug lines, with the season ending, Jaime felt like she owed it to Tad to share her feelings while there was still time. Even though she hadn't completely worked them out herself. "You asked me earlier…"

He interrupted her, reaching for her hands and taking the beer and vape away, setting them aside. Then he hauled her to her feet.

Facing each other, he looked her in the eyes, and his soft voice made her nervous. "Do you remember what you asked me?" When she hesitated, he lifted her chin and touched his lips to hers, softly, and as she leaned into the kiss, he groaned and dragged his mouth away.

"Yes, I want to."

"Oh… oh. Now?"

"Yes, exactly now." With one hand, he gently stroked the soft flesh along her ribs, nudging her T-shirt further and further up her ribcage, leaning down to lace his fingertip touches with soft kisses.

She laughed at him when he lost his balance and slipped sideways, but it didn't slow him at all. He sat on the rock and tugged her back down on his lap, still kissing the path back to her mouth.

She needed him to hurry as he pulled her close and his hands fumbled with her buttons. The air between them was thick with anticipation. She moaned as his callused fingers pushed the thin material of her bra out of the way and cupped her breast in his hand.

His touch flickered electricity through her body, and she wanted more, but she couldn't bear the idea of letting his mouth go.

Her fingers tugged impatiently on the button of his jeans, but then his hand found the crest of her nipple and she forgot what the hurry had been. He could never stop. He gently teased the hardened nipple, kissing her soundly the whole time, and she started wriggling, needing more. Or she was going to implode.

"Dad, Jaime! Where are you guys?"

She heard Ryan calling and her heart hit her stomach. They weren't supposed to be back yet. Tad groaned. What if they came looking for them? She jumped up and tried to put herself together, straightening her shirt, and trying desperately to look normal and calm her racing heart.

What a letdown.

She giggled, and he looked at her, a hurt expression.

"This is funny to you?" Tad asked.

"No, it's just I've never been almost caught by a kid before, and it's funny to me."

"You are one weird chick," said Tad. He gave her a kiss, then picked up her beer and vape and handed them back to her. He looked around for his hat and settled it back on his head with a shake.

"I guess they're back, so we better go see if they caught some fish." Tad looked so sad. She laughed again and popped him a good smack on his rear.

"We still have a week. Maybe we can fit it in."

He looked at her solemnly, his gray eyes troubled.

"We may have to take that as a sign it wasn't meant to be, my dear." He shook his head in defeat. "Shall we head back?"

It was her folks, so…

She sat around the campfire listening to her dad tell the kids the same stories that he'd told her and Jake when they were kids.

Having both her mom and Tad shoot her speculative glances all night long wasn't comfortable. Having the boys and the dog trying to crawl up in her lap was. Although they accepted her in the group, the feeling of not belonging to it was intimidating.

What was her end game?

Chapter 17

The dog was scratching at the door of the cabin. She felt sure
the boys had taught Hydro to do that because the dog made it
his daily mission to drag her up to the house, like she was a
newspaper or something.

"Go away," she mumbled, pulling the pillow over her head.
Jaime just wanted to go back to sleep and forget this was the big
day. That tomorrow it was done.

The reunion had been the topic on everyone's tongues for
almost a month now, and the pressure of it was too much. She
had no clue how she became so involved. It was far beyond her
obligation.

She got out of bed and let Hydro in. The large canine flashed
her a toothy grin and rested his head on her feet when she stood
in front of the coffee pot, patiently awaiting her daily dose of
energy.

There was a lot riding on today. Seeing her dad's excitement
at the thought of hosting his old company… the flood of
responses was unbelievable, and each acceptance had made him
even happier. Not only did she want Fall's Mill to thrive, she
also wanted her dad to see his dream come true.

As she sipped her coffee, she slipped into a swimsuit and
jeans, topped off with her Mom's hand dyed, red white and blue

tie dye, a special gift for the reunion. Seeing her mom and dad come together and work on their communication filled her with warmth. They worked through a lot of issues and had come out the other side. It must be a good year for forgiveness, because her dad seemed to have accepted her, too. Her twin was missing out.

She winced as she thought of Jake. Was she really going to leave Kat high and dry when her friend needed help with the one person only Jaime knew as well? She and Kat had just found common ground. She needed to think about that.

Booting the amorous hound off her sneakers, and pulling them on, she knew the day would be filled with excitement enough without looking for trouble. As she and Hydro stepped out on to the small porch, her day started with an unexpected twist.

Jaime knocked on the back door and poked her head into the kitchen at Tad's wave. "Hi, guys! I was just on my way out and I wanted to confirm game time today?"

Ry beamed at her and Cal asked, "Are you still going to watch us, Miss Jaime?"

"I wouldn't miss it for the world. We practically designed the entire day around you guys." She looked at Tad. "I think my folks are going to make it, too, though dad is already set up down at Falls Mill where he'll be storytelling and whittling the rest of the day, until the reenactment." She grinned. "You guys win big, then we're going to take a short float and be back in time for the show. I heard a rumor there may even be some fireworks afterward."

"Uhm, great." Tad didn't seem too thrilled. "The games at ten and everyone's welcome."

"Well, okay. I'll be there." She winked at Ry. "Keep your eye on the ball, right?"

"Right." His smile was killer, and she knew she was head over heels for this dude's kids. Who would ever have thought? She and Ry had been practicing catching pop flies for a week while Tad helped Cal with his batting, and both boys were feeling more confident.

"If I can hit the ball and make a run, Dad said I could try my bunt next time," Cal said. "That's really going to surprise them, huh?"

"You bet, sport. Good luck, boys. Coach." She winked at Tad and headed to the door. It was so normal here. After years of having someone else park her car for her at hotels, coming home to her cottage was a comforting thought. She often daydreamed about what it would be like to come home to a house full of family instead of her computer.

She thought about it more than she should.

"Jaime?"

"What's up, babe?" She hadn't noticed Tad follow her outside, but he stood nearly behind her as she turned from her car door. He smelled so good, fresh from the shower, but he had tired lines under his eyes, and she worried he wasn't getting enough help from her dad.

"Yeah…" He looked like he really didn't want to say what he had to say.

"The plan with Judith backfired a little—"

Just then, a silver Mercedes gleamed in the sunlight as it pulled into the yard and the perfect soccer mom stepped out.

"Ah." Tad cleared his throat and looked at the two women, looking like he was trying to wish himself away. "Judith, this is Jaime." His voice sounded strangled and if her heart hadn't cracked a little at how ideal this woman seemed, she would have laughed.

"It's nice to meet you, finally. You're the babysitter the boys speak so highly of. I think we spoke on the phone."

Jaime was speechless for a second. A deep blush climbed up her cheeks. She remembered her rude imitation of a hayseed, but that wasn't what had her buffaloed. She was used to taking crap for her jokes.

Judith looked perfect next to Tad. Like she belonged there. Where was the business suit and frosty exterior? She wore casual clothes in team colors and her perfectly highlighted blond locks gathered in a fashionable ponytail.

"Uhm, yes, I… I was watching the boys that day and—"

"Wonderful accent. I was worried Tad was undoing the kids' foundation of languages, but it turns out they're just enriched by comedic talent. That's wonderful, honey." She turned and put her hand on his so casually but possessively there was no mistaking it.

Tad was blushing himself and moved outside her reach, though not discouraging her. Exactly.

"Well, Jaime's not the boy's sitter," he said. "She's been staying in the cabin this summer while she helps my sister out at the resort, and she's been doing a little work around here, too."

A little. For real? She'd been breaking her back for six weeks for this cowboy and… whatever.

"How quaint," Judith said sweetly. "Like in the westerns, the ranch hand pays for room and board with labor. What a great idea! You could probably make more money, darling, if you rented this place out as a dude ranch. Too bad your sister beat you to it."

She looked at Jaime. "Well, we won't keep you, dear. I'm here to see the boy's last baseball game, but it sounds like I arrived at an enjoyable time. There's a big party for your sendoff. I'm so glad I got to meet the legend before you leave."

She turned to Tad. "I'd love to see the inside. I'm eager to see what you've accomplished. The outside is splendid with the scent of jasmine in the air. Are the children here?"

Tad looked meaningfully at Jaime, but she was too annoyed to cooperate. Again. The babysitter. Backfired.

She ducked back into her cabin and gathered a few things. If Judith stayed, she'd just bunk at her dad's. It was time someone cleaned her room out after all these years. She might as well do that before she left. She grabbed her computer and her bag and tossed them in the passenger seat. When she slammed her car door and drove off, she was really mad at herself.

She thought about water fights and playing catch with Cal and Ry in the house, even though it was against house rules. The dog had learned he could be on the furniture when she was around, and he was always climbing up in her lap. The kids did, too. A smile at the corner of her lips threatened to break through until she allowed the thought to continue. This was over, done, no more. She was leaving Riverbend Falls.

Love was for other people who weren't selfish and insensitive. Love was for people who deserved it by being ready to settle down and make babies and give up on personal dreams and goals. Jaime would never be that kind of girl.

That was her man, and she was handing him over.

She knew she couldn't keep him, so she should encourage them to rebuild their bond. She needed to finish this and be done. Her heart broke into a million pieces, and she pulled off to the side of the deserted dirt road to wipe away tears she hadn't realized were falling.

All these years, she had carried responsibility for an accident to avoid heartache. She carried the blame and insulated herself with it. Here, people all around her were cherishing life, not wasting it. Her folks were alive, working through years of silences and angry hurts to make a new life for themselves together. Who was she to throw away a chance at love?

"And the boys," she moaned to herself, and the tears threatened to flood her again. She did love them. There was no mistaking the fondness in her heart for them, frustration at Ry's sadness, the elation at Cal's growing success as he learned how to read despite suffering from some dyslexia no one had noticed. She loved them both… all. Even the big scary dog.

This was it. She was moving on in her mind right here. She was going to have to choose a path. Tomorrow, her unofficial contract was up. She was going to let Tad and his family move on without her. It would be okay.

She wondered if Judith knew Ry feared pop flies? Would she pet Hydro's ear fondly while she cheered for the home team? A tear leaked out just then, just one more, and Jaime wiped it away and knew.

No way did she cry over a man.

She was in a mess now, that was for sure. What could she do to fix this?

She took out her phone to call the shipping company that

faithfully moved her life from job to job and when she tried to dial them, she just stared at her phone, not noticing when the phone went dark to save power.

When she dialed, instead she called the cruise line that was waiting for a commitment from her. She wouldn't be making it.

No matter what happened now, she would not run away, leaving everyone she loved behind to wonder what happened to her. She took a deep breath and felt the resolution settle inside of her.

She was not going to run away from her heart.

But first, she had to survive this day. She called to make sure the tables and chairs were being transported to the side of the battlefield. Although it was expensive to have them delivered almost a hundred miles, the setup and breakdown crew provided a sense of security that made it worthwhile. She tapped her phone off and stepped out into the vibrant sunlight, feeling the heat on her skin.

The view from the Clubhouse office on the hill was almost as incredible as from the restaurant's deck. The tantalizing aroma of roasting pork filled the air. A girl could get used to this.

Perhaps she shouldn't have fought so hard. What was the worst thing that could happen? The best thing would be that she would hang her hat permanently in the bedroom of a handsome cowboy. Was she really going to help Judith? She wanted Tad for her own, and unless something had changed, this lady had already remarried. So, he was fair game.

She slipped in at the ball game, but she didn't get out of her car. She watched from the early morning shade at the edge of the field.

When Cal hit a double, she got out and cheered, and when Ry caught the game winning pop fly that got the other team out, she almost ran on the field she was so excited. Instead, she gave him a thumbs up and headed back down to the Mill. She'd tried not to notice Judith on the bleachers behind Tad, who was looking scrumptious coaching at first base. She'd given them a friendly wave, but stayed out of conversation range.

She needed a plan, and she knew who to turn to.

She'd seen Lana drive off half an hour ago, and she imagined her little worrier was checking on last-minute details at the resort, so she set to tracking down her best friend.

There hadn't been anyone manning the front desk, but there was a note explaining they'd be back after the game. The whole town was caught up in the boys' good luck. And she was alone with her thoughts. Lana's call echoed through the air, offering her a reprieve from her thoughts of despair and escape.

"Hey, I thought you were at the ball game…" Lana said. "I snuck out early to check on things here, but it's looking good."

She had been walking down suicide hill toward the restaurant when Lana's voice echoed across the space. Jaime felt her fight-or-flight trigger. She didn't want to examine her feelings about Judith sleeping in Tad's house, moving around his kitchen, cheering for the boys in her place. She was their mother, for heaven's sakes. That was what she was supposed to be doing.

And Jaime was supposed to help her friend using her talents, then get out of town. How had this gotten so screwed up?

Right. She didn't keep her libido in check.

She just stopped and sat on the steps of the restaurant and waited for Lana to join her.

"Judith came to stay with them, so I'm giving them plenty of space." Jaime exhaled slowly and stared out across the parking lot, then looked at Lana hopefully. "Maybe I could just move on a day early. I don't know what I'm saying, Lan. I already called and told the cruise line I was out. I'm thinking about staying for you, and I thought, maybe, but how can I get in the way if they are going to rebuild their family?"

Lana was looking at her strangely.

"Why would she come to Riverbend Falls? She hates it here." Lana sounded puzzled and annoyed all in the same breath.

Jaime started guiltily, remembering her meddling. It would serve her right if they patched up their relationship. "I suggested we invite her out so she could see there was culture here."

"Why?" Lana glared at her, somewhere to lay the blame now. "I thought you and Tad were becoming an item."

That almost did it, but Jaime held on to her composure. "It was a good idea. She was threatening to come get them and I convinced Tad if he would have her here, at the resort," she emphasized, "and maybe have a wine tasting or something. We could show her Riverbend Falls was a nice town to raise the boys in and that they wouldn't suffer horribly from a lack of culture."

Lana was surprised. "They wouldn't? I mean, of course they wouldn't. You really think we've brought a little culture to our sleepy town?"

"Sure," Jaime said, preoccupied. "At the town meetings, everyone's discussing the historical significance, personal heritage, you know. There's been a movement toward renovating a few other structures with history. I've heard Cal and Ry talking with their friends about wanting to work here when they grow up. Mom and Dad…"

Jaime trailed off. "Crap, my folks are going to be disappointed. They had designs on Cal and Ry."

"You packed already? So, you're not going to fight for my brother?"

Hesitating, Jaime said, "Well, it simplifies the goodbye scene tomorrow."

"What did Tad say?" Lana wanted to know and Jaime dipped her head guiltily again. "I didn't tell him yet."

"Hmmm…" Lana stood up, catching Jaime's hand. She hugged her friend. "If I know you, you're already trying to figure out how to move on. Why did you come here?"

"I thought I might work…"

"Jaime, what you've done for us is amazing. You took our idea and turned it from a funded plan into a growing operation. Have you considered staying on and running it for me? I could use you permanently, y'know." She patted her tummy. "Garrett's great, but he's no girlfriend."

"I'm thinking about it, but I'm not entirely sure…" Jaime's voice was pained. She was considering it, but what if Tad chose

Judith? Would she still be happy she stayed? "I've—"

"Never mind with the excuses, babe," Lana said coolly. "I've heard them all before. Are you ever going to stop running away from your feelings? If you're in love with my brother, why don't you go get him?"

"In love?" Jaime sputtered. "It may be true, but I haven't actually come to terms with the idea. One day, he jumped into my world, and it's not righted since. Maybe it's trauma love or something?"

Lana glared at her. "Dr. J, do you believe the jazz your spewing? You're spreading it on thick. You've been mooning around for weeks. I thought I heard wedding bells." Lana walked over to the landing that overlooked the river. "I thought we might have it right here, where you two first met. Lord knows we've had some real times together here on this riverbank."

"Maybe Judith…"

"Jaime." Lana's voice held a warning tone. "You know he doesn't love her, and she doesn't love him. She uses those children to hurt him and somehow, she's figured out a whole new way to manipulate him. Whatever possessed him to go along with your stupid plan, I'll never figure out, but we're not letting it go."

She blew at a short wisp of her blond hair that was blowing softly in the wind. "You're going to help me get rid of that woman before she destroys Tad again, and then if you want to run off with your tail tucked, that's your call. A wine tasting, huh? I guess poisoning her is out."

"Geez, Lana, be a little less brutal…" Jaime's feelings were hurt, but her friend always knew what to say. She reached out and gently touched the scar on Lana's cheek where she got cut in the car accident that took her folks. Then she gave her friend a good, long look and tapped her on the nose for luck. "So, what do I do, oh sage sister?"

"I guess… we use today to make sure your plan works perfectly. You're going to buddy up to her on the float and make sure she likes you. Then she won't care what he does as long as he pays her off. She can't think of you as competition. So you have to do what all stepmoms have to do, and make friends with the ex. For the children's best interest."

Jaime was shaking her head. "You are kidding. Tell me you are."

Lana smiled smugly. "Nope, unless you're interested in drinking wine with her. Now it's time to float and win over ex-wives. I suspect you can handle Tad on your own after that." With an outrageous laugh, Jaime realized she was doing this. She was glad she wore her one-piece swimsuit, she thought with a feisty grin.

"I couldn't have a better friend on all the earth. I am so glad you're mine."

"Back at ya, J. Now, get out of here. Dinner and a show for two hundred will be ready when you get back. Enjoy the fruits of your labors, you've earned it." Jaime left to change for the short two-mile float that might just be the ride of her life.

The float was exhilarating, she'd exuded so much charm, she'd apparently confused her boys, but Judith was eating out of her hand, and had made a few veiled suggestions she would happily help Jaime draw up the pre-nups, should there be any. Tad was distant, but it was for the best.

She thought sweetly of how Cal and Ry had played in their kayaks. Tad had taken a solo canoe since he was experienced, and he and a few other guys carried coolers of drinks and snacks for the nearly forty adventurous floaters who came.

He'd skillfully steered them down several rapids that had Jaime's blood quivering with excitement. She felt the powerful rumbling of the waves as they crashed close to her. The turtles sunning themselves had given the boys several stories, and she was quite enamored with the shy mud turtles herself.

The float was over too soon, but the adventure was still in full force. The food was a big hit. No one had seen a hog roasted in the ground in twenty years. That Garrett and Lug had pulled it off had everyone rolling full bellies to the next stage of entertainment. The reenactment was as short as the battle, but the old soldiers had all drawn numbers for their sides and played their parts with dignity and realistic aplomb.

She watched, fascinated, as Kat's Grandpa Eli was shot, and did a death throe Shakespeare would envy.

When Ralph Houston, the grocer, died by gunshot, she saw Vivian jump and run toward him, checking to see he'd taken the fall well, and he reached up and kissed her. She seemed surprised but pleased as she left him "wounded" on the battlefield.

Smiles all day long. Everyone was in a good mood. Lana and Garrett had provided the most excellent venue, and the whole day's events had gone well.

Until it was almost time for the fireworks.

Jaime collapsed next to her mom on a blanket, looking forward to the last part of the day. Judith left after dinner with a promise to friend Jaime, and Jaime considered it a win. Tad was still acting a little distant and weird, but she'd catch up with him soon.

"Thank you, Jaime." Her mom patted her shoulder, a mirror of her own turquoise eyes twinkling back at her from her mum's face. "Your dad has had an epic day, and I'll think he'll be talking about this for years to come."

Jaime followed her mother's gaze to where Tad and Lug were deep in discussion with Garrett's grandpa Jasper and Mr. Rosati as they rehashed the battle.

"Dad's acting weird. I know I've been away, so maybe it's not strange, but I can't remember him ever laughing so much." Jaime poked around in the picnic basket and was rewarded with a handful of chocolate chip cookies. "I feel like I've missed something."

"It's a surprise to me, too," Tabby admitted. "Since you came, and I came, several things changed all at once. What with the boys, and you and Tad, and—"

"Mom! You guys have to stop this. I don't know what the future holds, and you pushing me never works. His ex-wife was breathing down his neck today, and not to mention Cal and Ry. I can't imagine being a mom. I don't know how to handle kids."

Her tirade was abruptly halted by her mom's horrified expression, and when she looked up, she saw Ry behind her. No doubt he'd heard what she said, since his lip trembled.

"Oh no, Ry. Look, I know you heard that, but it's not exactly how I meant it. See…"

"It's okay, Miss Jaime. Our mom doesn't like us either. She forgot to say goodbye to us." He held out a paper parachute, one of the daytime fireworks she'd enjoyed watching as a child, and she recalled the promise she'd made to Cal and Ry just the week prior to get some for the fireworks show. "I got this for you, but it's stupid."

He dropped it on the blanket and walked away, toward a group of kids running pell-mell, throwing snapjacks and smoke bombs and chasing parachutes.

"Geez, Mom." Jaime gave her mom a pensive look. "I'll be back." She chased after Ry, reaching him at a big tree. "Hey kiddo, can I talk to you a minute?"

"I guess." His low, hollow tone didn't ease her worries, and she waved her hand in the direction of the tree.

"Can we sit down just a minute?" He didn't say anything, but sat rigidly next to her at the base of the old oak. "Ry, I'm sorry for what you heard there. I know what I said, and it wasn't exactly what I meant."

A breeze drifted across them, and Jaime wanted to kick herself. She could see tears shining in his eyes, and she'd done that by being selfish.

"See, I'm not good with short people usually." Oh great. His chin jutted out and she could tell things were not getting better, but she had to keep going. "But you and Cal, you're different. You know about baseball and fishing and hunting and all the kinds of cool things I like, so I have fun with you."

He was looking at her now and she was pretty sure he wasn't buying it, but his form had relaxed a bit. "Now see, littler kids… I guess it's not so much that I don't like them as much as I'm scared of them. Like when babies cry and want something but I can't figure out what it is, I kind of freak out."

Ry nodded slowly. "When our cow had a baby, I was scared,

but Dad helps make it okay." He picked up a green leaf off the ground, splitting up the vein the way Jaime always did when she was thinking. "But you don't want to be our mom."

"Well, see, really, I can't be. Your Dad and I—"

"Why don't you like Dad? He won't make you have babies if you don't want. When him and Mom yell at each other, he says it was her idea." A tear spilled down his cheek. "But Dad loves us and even if he didn't really want us, he still takes care of us. He thinks we're cool, too."

"You are so cool, Ry. I can't talk to you about the grown-up parts of this but—"

"What if we want you to stay, anyway? We don't have to call you Mom. Our Mom likes us to call her Judith. We could just call you Jaime."

Oh, good lord, how did parents handle this? "I tell you what sport. Why don't you let me and your dad discuss this, but I can tell you for sure, if I was really your mom, I would want you, and I would love you." She offered him a cookie, which he accepted, pushing the tears off his cheek.

"Okay. Can I sit by you for the fireworks?"

"Only if you can beat me back to the blanket." She nodded to where her mom was trying not to watch with concern.

"Are you sure you like us?" Ry was looking at the blanket as if gauging his route through the milling townsfolk, but he looked back at her for confirmation before getting up.

"I'm positive, sport. I like you and Ry real well." She was relieved as she scrambled to her feet to give Ry a sporting run back to where her Mom would know how to handle things from here. Whew, she was so not parent material. But she did okay.

Jaime looked around the restaurant. Empty now, but full just hours ago. Everything was done. The reservation system was working finally, the team was working together. The food was tasting good, being served hot, and the patrons were happy. The bar was working just as well. This was normally the time when Jaime's confidence soared. This was the turning point. She'd won, and the impact of her success was noticeable—a feeling of hope and possibility was in the air.

There were still a few wrinkles to iron out, and some long-term staff would need promotions before she left, people who would remain in place or float where needed, but Lana wouldn't need her much longer, so she was ultimately home free.

So why did she feel like… crying?

Tad had avoided her all night, and she was worried.

She leaned out over the porch railing on the deck, remembering the first time she'd seen the boys playing in the water. The beginning of the summer seemed so long ago.

Her eyes scanned the callouses she'd developed on her hands. She would miss… who was she kidding? She'd decided she wanted the Stone family as her own. That's what this was all about. She wanted to stay, but she'd set up every path to bat clear out of the field. And she hadn't told Tad she didn't want to leave.

"Then why don't you stay?"

His voice behind her had her jumping. She'd been alone. "How…?"

Tad leaned on the railing next to her. "You didn't lock the door, and I knew you'd be here, and I knew what you'd be thinking. Jaime, I know I went about everything with you wrong, but what was that today? Is everything a game to you? Were you making fun of Judith or bonding with her? I couldn't tell."

Ouch. Jaime leaned over beside him, her lips quivering and her heart full of sorrow. "I don't know how to be the person you need, Tad, the mother the boys need. All I know how to do is screw up my life and fix other people's problems." She grinned at him ruefully. "In my head, the doctor is out."

"You are already the woman we need. You don't have to change." He lightened his serious look with a soft smile. "The boys will nag you until the end of time about the dangers of vaping. And they're cleaning you out on the ole 'cussing' jar. We already love you, just the way you are."

"I want to believe that Tad, but this town reminds me of who I am, where I came from, the dumb decisions I've made, and, well, I don't always like me. I bring baggage, even though I travel light. My mood swings alone—"

Tad reached over and took her hand in his. "Are legendary. As is your temper, your quick thinking. Everything about you is almost too much, but then you settle just on this side of perfect. I won't beg you, Jasmine, because I have too much baggage myself, and two boys who count on me to make the right decisions for them. I want to trust your opinion when you say you're not right for us, because I trust your intuition. You know your mind and your heart. If you choose to leave us, I'll know it's because you believed it was true, but we'll always miss you. You're the one for us. We know it, and we aren't wrong about this one."

A tear leaked out of the corner of Jaime's eye. "I want to believe… look, maybe I just need a little more time."

"No!" He shook his head firmly. "No more stalling. The last thing you need is time. You already know you want us. I see it in your movements. I've watched you tuck Cal and Ry into bed, the longing that fleets across your features. I know you belong with us, and you know it. Time will give you the chance to desensitize. You'll aim to break away the same way, using the same tricks you used to move on from each of your jobs."

He kissed her on the nose. "Sweetheart, look at us. Love us. We love you. You'll love you at the end of every day when you see how we love you."

She just looked at him, frustration warring with desperation. "Tad, I…"

"Fine." He straightened, almost painfully, but there was no discernible expression on his tired face. "Well, sweetheart, it's been real. Drop us an email once in a while, huh?"

"Wait!" She couldn't breathe, but the thought of leaving them behind was unbearable. "What are you proposing, exactly, if I was hypothetically interested?"

He smiled at her, but not like she wanted him to. "That's where our troubles began," he said.

"Let's end them there. Let's see if we could make this work."

"I told you once, Jaime, it was all in or I am all out."

"Would you do me the honor of making an honest woman of me, Tad? Marry me?"

He looked at her a moment, and with a straight face, he asked, "Do you think I would marry you without taking you for a ride? I have to find out if my car approves of you. I'm parked out front."

She laughed, feeling truly happy to have met someone that got her. "Tad Stone, has anyone ever told you have no idea how to finesse a woman?" She arched her eyebrow at him.

Then he grinned at her, and took his hat off, and put it on her head backward. She got a kiss that let her know he liked her more than the car. He swept her into his arms and showered her with more kisses, and she knew for real, she was home.

When he came up for air, she looked at him in a bit of a daze.

He winked at her. "So, that's a yes. Vegas? Tomorrow? I'll drive."

"If we can bring the kids and convince your sister, it's a done deal."

Delilah Dewey spends her small hours of the morning crafting genuine tales of small-town romance, before leaving for her fulfilling day job as a Trust department secretary. She loves to immerse herself in the research process, exploring every detail.

When she isn't working at a computer, or spending quality time with her own romantic hero, she can be found cuddled up to a book, soaking up the warmth of the season, or donning her boots and gloves and tackling whatever tasks present themselves.

Delilah loves outdoor activities, like camping in a tent near the river, admiring the wildlife, and enjoying a warm campfire in the evening.

Books written by Delilah Dewey

Published by Delilah's Diction

Lana's Leap

Planting Jasmine

Visit my Author Page on

Facebook or Amazon,

or visit my website at

delilahsdiction.com